THE BLUE MEDALLION

CLAUDE ANTHONY GOSSMAN

authorHOUSE®

AuthorHouse™
1663 Liberty Drive
Bloomington, IN 47403
www.authorhouse.com
Phone: 1 (800) 839-8640

Published by AuthorHouse   10/12/2016

ISBN: 978-1-5246-4462-8 (sc)
ISBN: 978-1-5246-4461-1 (e)

Library of Congress Control Number: 2016916945

Print information available on the last page.

DEDICATION

I dedicate this book to my beautiful

Janice; and to my second love – my

wombmate– my Twin– Claudette; and

finally, to the memory of our wonderful

son Jeffrey Thomas Gossman . A son

so generous, thoughtful, caring and

devoted and thoroughly missed . May

he rest in peace within God's love !

Claude Anthony Gossman

CONTENTS

FORWARD.

As a young youth, back about 1945 - just as the war was getting over, I remember looking up at the full moon in the clear, dark sky. I was impressed at how bright it was - how it seemed so close - yet so far away. In my wildest imagination, I could never of even thought, that a human from earth, would actually walk on it's surface.

I'm learning that the brain and mind is capable of some far fetched concepts, that present day thinking is not even able to imagine. Our God has provided us with capabilities that are second only to His Son and Himself.

In Chapter 4, the verbage may seem far removed from reality and maybe it is. But I believe if you can imagine it - if you can think it -then it must be possible - some day !

The characters in this book are caring, thoughtful, generous and helpful, for the most part. The exception being the Dober boys.

As the author, I find it truly amazing, of what the mind can concieve - considering that these stories were written, back in 1972. I'm just beginning to put the book together now, in 2013.

To those reading this book, with an open mind, I think that they will get maximum enjoyment and benefit from these stories - especially from Chapter Six.

God Bless !

The Author

Historical Background of Blue Medallion

Medallion came from outer spacecraft patroling the Planet " Borderia " located in the Andromeda Galaxy.

" Borderia " was smashed by a colliding Star and blew into a million pieces. The concussion destroyed the spacecraft.

polished and formed by speeding thru hundreds of solar particle streams

medallion markings were part of sacred writings used to worship the Supreme Being.

Black Sun emblem indicates planet "Borderia " was on back side of sun

remnant was Brain of Planet " Borderia "

Composition of the Medallion

Pure grade of raw corundum asbestos galena gold with outer ridge encrusted with pure platinum with corundum sapphire gemstone embedded in center of medallion.

four pins formed by millions of electrons pounding against the metal
size reduced from 200 feet in diameter to 3 inches in diameter
heated to more than one million degrees for three hundred years
entered a complete vaccum
cooled to a temperature of ten thousand degrees below zero

Note: Drited in space - caught in a heatstream from Earth space
         vehicle - pulled into Earth's gravititational pull and plummeted
         into the Golf of Mexico near Huston Texas.

THE BLUE MEDALLION

JAKE SCOBEY HURRIED THROUGH THE BUSY HOUSTON BUSINESS SECTION CARRYING A BRIEFCASE AT HIS SIDE. HE WAS TO DROP OFF THE BRIEFCASE BEFORE 8:00 AM AT THE PLAZA CONVENTION CENTER, WHERE HIS BOSS WAITED IMPATIENTLY FOR HIS ARRIVAL.

HE HAD BEEN WITH THE FIANANCIAL PLANNING SERVICES CO. FOR FIVE YEARS NOW AND HAD BEEN TOLD, WHEN HE WAS HIRED, THAT IF HE WORKED HARD AND WAS DEDICATED TO HIS WORK, THAT HE WOULD BE ABLE TO PROGRESS RAPIDLY UP THE LADDER OF UPPER MANAGEMENT.

HE GLANCED AT THE BIG SHINY CADILLAC AS IT PASSED HIM AND HE ENVIED ITS DRIVER. THAT GUY HAD IT MADE HE THOUGHT AS HE HURRIED ALONG THE STREET. AT A STOPLIGHT, HE WAITED IMPATIENTLY FOR THE CHANGING LIGHT AMONG THE CROWD. HE FELT SOMETHING HIT HIS LEG AND HE LOOKED DOWN AT A DROPPED WALLET. HE GLACED AT THE WOMAN BESIDE HIM WHO WAS SORTING THROUGH HER PURSE, FINALLY FINDING HER CAR KEYS. LEANING DOWN, HE PICKED UP THE WALLET AND QUICKLY HID IT IN THE NEWSPAPER THAT HE CARRIED. THE LIGHT CHANGED AND THE CROWD SURGED AHEAD. HE HEADED INTO THE CONVENTION CENTER, STUFFING THE WALLET INTO HIS JACKET POCKET.
HE DROPPED THE BRIEFCASE OFF TO HIS BOSS AND HURRIED AWAY, SMILING TO HIMSELF; HE WAS FREE FROM HIS BOSS FOR TWO WEEKS WHILE HIS BOSS ATTENDED BUSINESS MEETING OUT ON THE WEST COAST.
HE RESENTED HIS BOSS, HIS BIG MONEY TALKS AND HIS FLEET OF BIG CARS.

SOME DAY, JAKE SCOBY WAS GOING TO BE SOMEBODY....
AND SOON! HE WOULD NOT MAKE THE SAME MISTAKES HIS BOSS
MADE. SHARING ALL THE PROFITS WITH THE EMPLOYEES. THEY
ALL EARNED A PAYCHECK EACH WEEK. WHY WASTE MONEY ON A
YEARLY BONUS WHEN IT COULD BE INVESTED AND EARN, STILL
MORE MONEY. HIS THOUGHTS WERE INTERUPTED BY A WOMAN
FLAGGING DOWN A TAXI CAB. AS THE CAB PULLED UP NEXT TO
THE CURB, HE QUICKLY STEPPED IN FRONT OF HER AND HOPPED
INTO THE BACK SEAT. THE DRIVER SHRUGGED HIS SHOULDERS
AND PULLED OUT INTO THE MOVING TRAFFIC.
JAKE REMEMBERED THE WALLET IN HIS JACKET POCKET AND
GLANCED THROUGH IT. FIFTY-SIX LOUSY BUCKS! OH WELL...FREE
TO HIM. HE PULLED OUT THE CREDIT CARDS AND SHOVED THEM
INTO HIS POCKET. INSURANCE CARDS, DRIVER'S LICENSE, DONOR
CARD AND A MEDICAL ALERT CARD FOR INSULIN. HE THREW THEM
OUT THE SIDE WINDOW, GLANCING AT THE DRIVER TO SEE IF HE
SAW HIM, BUT THE DRIVER WATCHED THE HEAVY TRAFFIC IN
FRONT OF HOM. JAKE SLID THE EMPTY WALLET INTO THE BACK OF
THE SEAT. AT HIS DETINATION, HE PAID THE DRIVER AND HURRIED
DOWN THE STREET.
HE STOPPED IN FRONT OF A ROUGH LOOKING CHARACTER
LEANING AGAINST A WALL AND HANDED HIM THE CREDIT CARDS.
THE SURPRISED CHARACTER TOOK THEM AND THANKED HIM, BUT
JAKE WAVED HIM OFF AND HURRIED AWAY.

DOWN IN THE GULF OF CALIFORNIA, A FISHING VESSEL OUT
OF LOS MOCHIS SAT ANCHORED IN THE CHOPPY WATERS OF THE
SEA. THEIR DIVERS SEARCHED UNDERWATER FOR CLAMS, CRABS,
SHELLFISH AND SEAWEED. THEY PLACED THE CRAB TRAPS INTO
NETS ALONG WITH CLAM BASKETS AND THE SEAWEED BASKETS.
TUGGING ON THE BOOM ROPES, THE NETS WERE LIFTED ONTO
THE WAITING FISHING VESSEL THE BOOM OPERATOR SWUNG THE
NETS TO THE BINS AND RELEASED THE NETS.

At the end of the day, the fishing vessel headed back to its home port of Los Mochis. Several workers on board had sorted the seaweed from the crabs , clams and shellfish and tossed the seaweed into their cartons. This successful fishing catch would be taken to a fish market in Houston.

Jake went into a back alley and stepped into the back door of a big seafood processing center and stopped in the processing room where his friend was sorting seaweed for packaging. The phone rang in the background and his friend went to answer the phone. Jake looked down at the processing table and picked off a piece of seaweed. As he did, something glittered in the seaweed and he picked up a metal coin or medallion and looked at it, quickly stuffing it in his pocket. He hurried past his friend, slapping him on the back. " I can't wait… wasn't that important…catch you later ". Outside, he looked at the coin or medallion, wondering what it was. He had to hurry home and shower and shave to get ready for his date with Cindy. He wished he was home and ready for his date. Instantly, it happened and he was home and in his shower. He sat on his bed trying to analize what had just happened. A moment ago, he had been blocks away and now he was home, refreshed, fully dressed and ready for his date. I wish I knew what was happening he thought. The medallion immediately warmed and a blue glitter beamed up at him. This thought popped into his head and he knew that this coin or medallion gave him his wishes. Okay - I wish I had a handful of one- hundred dollar bills. The medallion warmed in his hand and he looked down at his other hand . It was filled with a stack of hundred dollar bills.

" HOT DAMN " HE SAID ALOUD.

DRESSED IN FRESH CLOTHES, HE KNOCKED ON CINDY'S DOOR. SHE OPENED THE DOOR AND HE SMILED AT HER. "READY CINDY? " HE ASKED. SHE NODDED. "CINDY, CAN YOU LOAN ME TWENTY DOLLARS ? I'M A LITTLE SHORT THIS WEEK...I'LL PAY YOU BACK NEXT WEEK". SHE NODDED. "SURE JAKE. BUT YOU ALRADY OWE ME TWO-HUNDRED DOLLARS ...THAT YOU HAVEN'T PAID ME BACK YET". "HEY...YOU'LL GET PAID NEXT WEEK...DON'T YOU TRUST ME? I TOLD YOU...I'M A LITTLE SHORT THIS WEEK...YOU DO WANT TO GO OUT AND EAT WITH ME DON'T YOU?" CINDY NODDED HER HEAD, NOT BEING REALLY SURE, BUT SHE HANDED HIM A TWENTY.

AT THE HMBURGER JOINT DOWN THE STREET, CINDY SAID "I THOUGHT THAT WE WERE GOING OUT TO EAT?" "WHAT DO YOU THINK THIS PLACE IS , A SHOE STORE?" WALKING UP TO THE COUNTER, HE ORDERED A HAMBURGER, SMALL ORDER OF FRIES AND A SMALL DRINK FOR HER AND A LARGE ORDER OF FRIES, TWO CHEESEBURGERS AND A LARGE DRINK FOR HIMSELF. HE PAID THE ATTENDANT WITH THE TWENTY, SHOVING THE CHANGE INTO HIS POCKET. THE FOOD WAS DELIVERED TO THEM AT THE CORNER TABLE. "LOOK CINDY, SOMETHING REALLY IMPORTANT HAS COME UP AND I HAVE TO CUT OUR DINNER DATE SHORT...OKAY" HE ASKED. " SURE JAKE....BUT I THOUGHT THAT WE WERE GOING OUT TO SOME NICE PLACE TO EAT AND DANCE?" SHE ASKED.
HE SMILED AT HER AS HE GULPED HIS FOOD. "WE WILL....I PROMISE...MAYBE NEXT WEEK...HURRY AND EAT BABE...I GOTTA RUN". IN LESS THAN AN HOUR, CINDY WAS BACK HOME IN HER APARTMENT AGAIN.

Jake walked down the street and as he passed by each business, he wished that all the money in the vaults or cash registers would appear in the large sacks he carried with him. In several moments the sacks were overflowing with coins and 'greenbacks'. Maybe he should wish for a car...a nice shiny black Cadillac and he did. Instantly. The car appeared at the curb beside him. Climbing in. He grinned to himself.

He drove from one block to another, parking at the curb as he made his wishes. Wishing for all the money in all of the business's on both sides of the street. When a bank was in the block, he really cleaned up and made a large haul. Arriving at his apartment, his whole car was loaded with paper money and coins. Wishing the contents in the car into his apartment, he stacked the paper money into stacks of one's, five's, ten's, twenties', fifties and one-hundred dollar bills. Grinning to himself, he considered what his activities would be for the next day. He would wish himself, all of his money and his car to a very high rent district...in fact he would do it right now.

He wished that he was at the most plush, extravgant motel complex in Houston, In the best suite. In an instant, he was in a eight room suite and the decor was spectacular. Down at the desk, he explained that he had lost his key and asked for a replacement. "Yes sir...Mr. Scoby...I'll get you another..right away sir. I hope the suite meets your approval...its the best in the house sir". Jake smiled at the clerk. "Oh it does...its fine..I like it very much". Jake left abruptly.

OUTSIDE IN THE GARDEN PATIO AND POOL AREA, HE MADE HIMSELF COMFORTABLE AT A PATIO TABLE. HE GLANCED AT THE PEOPLE THROUGHOUT THE POOL LOUNGE TABLES, AWARE OF THE WATCHES AND JEWELRY THAT EVERYONE WAS WEARING. HE WISHED THAT ALL OF THE JEWELRY, WATCHES AND RINGS WOULD APPEAR IN HIS MOTEL ROOM. A WELL DRESSED WOMAN NEARBY BEGAN TO SHRIEK AND SCREAM THAT SHE WAS MISSING HER NECKLACE AND RINGS. THEN EVERYONE IN THE POOL AREA BEGAN TO HOLLER AND SCREAM THAT THEIR JEWELRY, RINGS AND WATCHES WERE GONE. JAKE CALMLY FINISHED HIS GIN AND TONIC AND WALKED OVER TO THE DOORWAY AT THE ENTRANCE OF THE TERRACE. SECURITY HAD BLOCKED OFF THE AREA AND MADE THOROUGH SEARCHES OF EVERYONE. JAKE REMOVED HIS SHOES FOR THE REQUESTED SEARCH. UPON COMPLETION, HE HEADED FOR HIS ROOM.

BACK IN HIS ROOM, HE LOCKED HIS DOOR AND CLOSED THE CURTAINS, SMILING AT THE STACK OF JEWELRY ON THE RUG. HE WISHED THAT THE ITEMS WERE IN A SACK AND WERE IN THE TRUNK OF HIS CAR OUTSIDE. HE LEFT THE MOTEL COMPLEX AND HEADED TOWARDS HIS CAR. CHECKING HIS TRUNK, SATISFIED WITH THE SACK AND CONTENTS, HE CLIMBED INTO HIS CAR AND LEFT.

THE NEXT DAY, HE SAT IN HIS CAR, NEAR A BUSY INTERSECTION AND WISHED THAT ALL OF THE MONEY AND JEWELRY THAT PEDESTRIANS, DRIVERS AND RIDERS CARRIED, WOULD APPEAR IN HIS TRUNK.
BACK IN HIS ROOM, THE CONTENTS OF THE SACK PLEASED HIM. HE THOUGHT ABOUT HIS NEXT ADVENTURE AND DECIDED THAT IT WOULD BE FUN AND EXCITING, IF HE BECAME INVISIBLE, SO HE MADE HIS WISH.

NOW INVISIBLE, IN A SMALL DINER, HE REMOVED 85
CENTS OFF THE COUNTER, WHERE AN ELDERLY WOMAN SAT.
SHE HAD ORDERED A BOWL OF SOUP AND CRACKERS. SHE
LOOKED OVER THE COUNTER AND ON THE FLOOR FOR HER
MONEY. NOT FINDING IT, SHE LEFT, WONDERING WHERE SHE
WOULD GET HER NEXT MEAL. INSIDE THE DINER, JAKE WAS
HAVING A BALL. A BITE OF A SANDWHICH HERE; AND A SIP OF
COFFEE THERE. HE HELPED HIMSELF TO MALTS, BITES OF
CAKE AND PIES. WHILE A MOTHER TOOK HER YOUNG
DAUGHTER TO THE RESTROOM, JAKE HELPED HIMSELF TO HER
STEAK SANDWHICH AND ATE THE LITTLE GIRL'S BANANA
SPLIT.

AS THE MONTHS PASSED, JAKE PURCHASED ONE
APARTMENT COMPLEX AFTER ANOTHER WITH HIS WEALTH AND
HIS BANK ACCOUNTS INCREASED TEN FOLD DAILY. HE RAISED
THE RENT ON ALL OF THE TENANTS AND WHEN THEY
COULD'NT PAY THE RENT, HE THREW THEM OUT INTO THE
STREET.
HE CONTINUED TO BORROW FROM CINDY UNTIL SHE GREW
SICK OF HIM AND ORDERED HIM OUT OF HER APARTMENT. HE
IMMEDIATELY THREW HER OUT OF THE APARTMENT COMPLEX
THAT HE HAD RECENTLY PURCHASED.
HE WAS IN HIS OWN WORLD NOW AND HE COULD HAVE
ANYTHING HE DESIRED. HE COULD GO ANYWHERE HE DESIRED
AND HE DID SO DAILY. ROME, BERLIN, TOKYO, BOMBAY, NEW
YORK, BOSTON, LOS ANGLES, PHOENIX AND FINALLY LOS
VEGAS. HE REALLY CLEANED UP IN THE GAMBLING CITY.

HE COULD HAVE ANYTHING THAT HE WANTED…ANYTHING
THAT HE WANTED IN HIS WHOLE LIFE. WHAT DID HE WANT TO
BE? PRESIDENT? A KING? A RULER OF HIS OWN ISLAND?
MAYBE HE WOULD BE A RULER OF THE UNITED STATES. HE
LAUGHED TO HIMSELF.

HE WAS A GOD. HE OWNED EVERYTHING. ANYTHING HE WANTED WAS HIS…JUST FOR THE TAKING…OR THE WISHING. HE LAUGHED OUT LOUD.

SEVERAL DAYS LATER, HE DROVE THROUGH THE COLORADO MOUNTAINS, AT THIS LATE HOUR OF THE NIGHT. HE WAS CONTENT WITH HIMSELF AT HIS LATEST DISCOVERY; HE NEVER GOT SLEEPY OR TIRED. ALL HE HAD TO DO WAS WISH THAT HE NEVER GOT TIRED OR SLEEPY. "I AM A GOD… ALL POWERFUL" HE SAID TO HIMSELF. " MAYBE I'LL START MY OWN RELIGION LIKE JESUS CHRIST DID". HE LAUGHED LOUDLY TO HIMSELF.

AS HE CAME DOWN THE STEEP, CURVY, WINDING MOUNTAIN ROAD, HE HIT SOMETHING IN THE ROAD AND BOTH FRONT TIRES BLEW OUT. THE CAR BUMPED AND SWAYED AND THE MEDALLION, SITTING ON THE SEAT BESIDE HIM, FLEW TO THE RIDER SIDE OF THE FLOOR. HE REACHED FOR THE MEDALLION BUT IT WAS OUT OF HIS REACH. HE SLAMMED ON HIS BRAKES BUT NOTHING HAPPENED. THE STEEP DOWNGRADE PULLED AT HIS CAR AND HE LEANED OVER , REACHING FOR THE MEDALLION. THE ROAD CURVED SHARPLY AND HE SMASHED THROUGH THE GUARDRAIL AND HIT THE TIP OF A PINE TREE, TIPPING AND ROLLING THE CAR OVER IN THE AIR TO THE BOTTOM OF THE CANYON, TEN THOUSAND FEET BELOW. THE FULL GASTANK EXPLODED ON IMPACT AND A HUGE FIREBALL LIT UP THE DARK FOREST. THE FIRE FED ON THE ENORMOUS AMOUT OF PAPER MONEY IN THE TRUNK AND EVERYTHING BURNABLE DID. THE INDESTRUCTABLE MEDALLION FLEW INTO THE BACK AND UNDER THE BACKSEAT AND EVERYTHING THAT WAS BURNABLE WAS DESTROYED.

IN THE EARLY MORNING HOURS, A DRUNK CRASHED THROUGH THE SAME BROKEN GUARDRAIL AND LANDED ON

TOP OF THE SAME PINE TREE. THE CAR CAUGHT IN THE TOP OF THE TREE, BETWEEN THE BRANCHES. THE SUDDEN STOP AND JOLT THREW THE DRUNK INTO THE STEERING WHEEL COLUMN AND HE DIED INSTANTLY.

IN THE MORNING, STATE TROOPERS AND A WRECKER PULLED THE CAR OFF THE TOP OF THE TREE AND ONTO THE ROAD AND LEFT. LATER THAT DAY, THE GUARDRAIL WAS REPAIRED AND THE AREA WAS FORGOTTEN.

THE ARCHAEOLOGIST

The 1954-1955 school year drew to a close at the Inter-Mountain City College, located in the foothills of the Rocky Mountains and Marla Rowler hurried from the classroom. As she walked the six

blocks to her apartment, she sighed with relief, now that the long school year was over.

She was free for two weeks, until June 1, when she would begin the last segment of her Graduate work in Archaeology and by the end of summer, she would have her Doctorate Degree. Then in the Fall, ,she would join her father's expedition over in the Nile Valley, near Giza. She loved the teaching of Ancient History and about Ancient Civilizations, but it was not her first love. She preferred to be with her father and would have been, if he had not talked her into finishing her graduate work first. She had promised him, that she would complete her Degree work and would then, happily, join him in the Fall, to pursue her first love; digging in the rocks and sand, out in the hot, arrid wastelands of the Arabian Desert. To search and try to pull together, mysteries of great civilizations from centuries before. To participate in digging among sacred grounds - this was her first love.

She had not been with her father during his first discovery, nearly thirty years ago, when he had discovered a long, lost tomb of an Egyptian ruler. The pieces of the puzzle were still being investigated and put together, to this very day. The discovery was believed to be the tomb of Meriapen. Any day now, she expected to hear from her father, of the final proof, that the tomb had been correctly identified. Her father was expected to start a new search for another tomb in the Valley of Kings, believed to be five miles further West, from his last dig and she would join that expedition.

She planned to leave immediately, for the Southern region of the Colorado Rockies for a short, hopefully, sucessful search for a mysterious blue light that appeared on occasion, during the nights. The area had been searched thoroughly many times without success.

Two students of hers, had been deer hunting in the region last Fall. They had become lost in a sudden, unexpected snowstorm and were lucky to be found in the sub-zero temperatures. They had been spotted from the air by a search party and the helicopter had landed nearby, picking them up. The helicopter rose above the massive, dark forest just before darkness and the two rescued students had looked down at the darkening forest and had spotted a bluish light gleeming at them. Convincing the pilot of the sighting, he circled the area, but they saw nothing.

The rumors of the light continued but nothing was ever found. The two students had returned to the area later and scouted the whole area, but they were unsuccessful.

That had been three years ago and they had forgotten about it, until a class discussion on unusual sightings, and the strange blue light subject came up again.

Marla was becomming extremely curious of this blue light, having read about it in newspapers and magazines and local rumors. The area of the sightings was within fifty miles of her home and she had decided that she would spend several weeks in the heavily timbered area, searching for this mysterious blue light, in an effort to solve this puzzle, once and for all. There were those that said that it was part of a meteorite or a star; others said that it was part of an outer space vehicle. She didn't know what it was, or whether she would ever find out, but she intended to try.

Marla quickly changed clothes and left the apartment promptly, dressed in her grubby clothes and hiking boots. She had packed the night before and she placed the last box of her gear into the four wheel drive Jeep and drove to Montrose, arriving there after darkness. She checked into the motel, showered and ate a quick meal, before retiring for the night. At daybreak, she headed east toward Monarch and in a short time, she parked her Jeep on an old abandoned logging road in the heavily timbered forest. She set up her tent and camp quickly and began to explore the heavily wooded terrain. She made her way through the sage brush, scrub oak, pine and spruce trees toward the highest point in the area. From there, she looked over the tops of the trees, looking for anything out of place, but saw nothing.

She had searched the complete area for ten days now and had not found any clue to the light that she searched for. She broke camp and drove to a bluff, overlooking a deep canyon of forest on the other side of the pass and she set up her camp at the top of a mountain peak; the highest in the area. The sun dipped below the nearby mountain peaks and she decided to wait until morning, before she would begin her search of the bottom of the canyon.

That night, she sat on a boulder near her tent, near the rim of the canyon and looked through her infrared binoculars, glassing the area, looking for the blue light, but saw nothing.

She sipped at her cup of coffee and looked down into the dark canyon, far below her, wondering what the blue light was and what it meant. She smiled to herself. Maybe she was chasing a hoax or a false rumor. Well, she would hunt through the bottom-land tomarrow and then head back to the college, to prepare for her summer classes.

It was nearly midnight before the noise from passing cars and trucks quieted down and she was relieved by the peace and quiet of the cool, dark night. The steep incline of the road caused trucks to change gears noisily and the engines of the trucks roared, to climb the steep grade, or to hold the trucks at a slower speed on the way down, so as to not surge ahead too fast and cause a disastrous accident at the hair-pin turn, half-way down the steep mountain road.

She'd pour herself, one more cup of coffee and then retire for for the night. She turned the camping stove off and then shut down the kerosene latern. She loved sitting in the cool, dark woods, alone, collecting her thoughts.

Her coffee had cooled down and as she emptied her coffee over the rim of the canyon, something caught her eye and she looked again, but saw nothing. She knew that she had seen something and she picked up her binoculars and slowly and carefully scanned the bottom of the canyon. There.....what was that?... she thought and she moved the glasses back. Something glowed softly, disappeared and then re-appeared. The fir tree branches must be moving in front of it with the light breeze blowing she thought.

She made a mental note of the location and would look the area over in the morning. It was too steep and dangerous to attempt to go down in the dark. She promptly crawled into her warm sleeping bag.

Early the next morning, after a hearty breakfast of eggs, hashbrowns, sausage and black coffee, she headed down the steep slope.

She searched the area thoroughly, without success, only having found an old burnt out automobile, from years before and was ready to give up the search, when she decided to move her camp to the bottom of the canyon. She would spend one more night near the burnt out automobile. Maybe she would be able to spot the mysterious blue light from here, she thought.

She overslept from her afternoon nap, as she had waited for darkness and it was late into the evening, when she awoke. She tied a flashlight to her belt and worked herself up the trunk of a spruce tree, almost to the top. She looked down, searching for the blue light in the dark night. She spotted it almost immediately, right below her..... in the burnt out automobile?.... she wondered. She looked inside the wreckage of the overturned car and shut off her flashlight. There... under the springs of the back seat, lay a small, soft, glimmering blue light. What could it be? The light was so small and such a soft glow, that she wondered, how anyone could have seen it and how it had started such a rumor throughout the area.

She climbed over the framework of the front seat and shown her flashlight at the object. "A gold coin?" she said aloud and picked it up. "Sure is heavy" she said. She headed back to her camp, where she thoroughly examined the coin or medallion.

She was satisfied that she had found the source of the blue light and she watched the coin's blue glow in the dark, thoroughly facinated by the soft, blue glimmer. She picked it up, turning it over and over as she examined it. Some sort of hieroglyphic symbols or inscriptions on the coin, she thought.

What could it mean? What was it's purpose? Where had it come from? She wished that she knew what it did, or what it was good for. The coin in her hand grew warmer and in an instant, she had this feeling, that the beholder of this medallion was granted wishes.

Why did she have this strange feeling in her mind? She was puzzled by it and pondered over her thoughts.

Questioning her thoughts, she decided to ask for a wish - just to see what happen - if anything. "I wish...uh...for a hot pot of coffee" she said and looked over at the empty coffeepot, sitting on the cold cookstove. She walked over to the pot and picked up the coffeepot, not using the handle, but instead, wrapped her fingers around the metal pot and picked it up. "Ouch....damn it" she cried out and dropped the coffeepot. The liquid poured over the cold ground and steamed in the cold air. "Impossible!" she said aloud. She made the same wish again. She poured herself a cup of hot coffee and was really baffled by this strange medallion.

She wish that she was packed up and just arriving back at the college, as she hated the long drive back. The medallion warmed in her hand and she stared at it in facination. In an instant, she was driving her car right in front of her apartment. She quickly swerved to the curb and slammed on her brakes, causing people, passing by on the sidewalk, to look at her with curiosity. "Get ahold of yourself, Marla" she said aloud. She held her head in her hands as she tried to think this out. Was she finally, losing her mind? She turned around in her seat and leaned into the back of the Jeep. Everything was there! Her tent, cookstove, latern; all of her gear was there!

She held the medallion in her hand and wondered. "Okay…we're going to find out right now!" she said. "I wish all the street lights would go out" and they did. "I wish that they would all come back on" and they did.

"I wish that all my gear was inside my apartment" she said and it disappeared right in front of her. She hurriedly locked her car and ran up the stairs to her apartment. Inside, her gear sat on the floor, near the door. "Wow.... this is unreal Marla" she said, as she brushed her short blond hair back from her face. She sat on the couch and looked about the room. "I wish that this room was re-painted with new paint.... baby blue/gray walls and with an off-white ceiling; the bathroom walls.... painted with light blue and a misty white ceiling; my bedroom... I wish... had an off-white ceiling and the walls, wall- papered with a multi- colored wallpaper with imprinted historical figures on it". When she looked at the rooms, they were just as she had wished.

"I wonder what else I can do with this medallion? I wish I had more money than I could carry". Money immediately fell into her hands and soon, she stood in a pile of hundred dollar bills.

Again, she considered what she could do with this medallion. In a minute, she decided to try something else. "I wish that I could go back to the time of the Crucifiction of Jesus Christ.... as long as I can get back to this time period... and that I can take this medallion with me. The medallion got warm and in an instant, she stood on a dirt and rocky road on the outskirts of a small village. Nearby, she heard the low murmur of a crowd chanting some- thing in a foreign language, as they drew nearer. She wished ... let my ears hear the language in english and if I speak, let my mouth speak in that language. In a minute, the crowd surged closer and she could understand what they were shouting. "Crucify Him! .... Crucify Him! If you are God... save your- self" the crowd yelled at Him". There was a sharp "Crack" and she saw the rope snap across His back and He fell near her feet. He had a crown of thorns on His head and His hair was dark with dried blood. Blood ran down His cheeks and from His mouth. His back and legs were welted with rope whip burns. The Roman soldiers glared at her and pushed Him away from her and the crowd surged by her and pushed her into the background. She looked at herself and was grateful that she was dressed in the native clothing of the day. She looked down at her hand and saw that the medallion was still there and she ran ahead and caught up with Jesus. She pushed her way through the crowd and stood with her back to posts mounded in the ground and in front of the soldiers and they stopped the procession. "Wait...don't do this...you're making a big mistake" she said to a soldier. He glared at her and shouted at her "get out of the way woman or you'll feel the bite of this whip - out of the way". She wished that he would go soak his head in a bucket of water and the soldier ran off, in search of a bucket of water. She stood, face to face with Jesus and she trembled at the peace, love and tranquility on His face. She wiped His forehead with her scarf, but nothing changed. It was like she had not even wiped His face. She wished that He was not here...that He was safely outside the village and not near this inflamed crowd. Jesus looked at her with soft, loving and understanding eyes and smiled at her. Her mind had a message that immediately flashed into her senses. You cannot change what cannot be changed. Only My Father or I can change this...the medallion has no more power than My Father will allow it to have....Peace be with you and in your heart. Her mind went blank and the crowd pushed past her, towards the posts. She heard the terrible pounding as nails were pounded into Jesus, as He was nailed to the cross-member and erected into place.

She heard Him moan with pain and she wept. How can this be true.....
isn't there something that I can do - to help Jesus, she thought. Her
mind immediately filled with the word - NO!! and then....live your life
as He has commanded. She saw both Mary's at the foot of the cross and
Marla walked over near Mary, the Mother of Jesus and watched Her weep.
Even in heart breaking sorrow, this woman was the most beautiful woman
that she had ever seen.

Marla glanced over the crowd and she was sure that one of the bearded
men that peered, from beyond the crowd, was an Apostle...probably Peter.
Marla was horrified... here she st o o d, in front of the greatest man that
ever lived... and He was suffering and being put to death.... right in front
of her eyes.... and her medallion was of no help. She stood at the foot of
the cross and looked up at Him. I wish that there was somthing that I
could do, she thought. Jesus raised His head and looked down at her and
then spoke to His Mother. " Mother....behold thy son....son....behold thy
Mother". When Jesus had looked at her, her mind recieved a message.
Woman...thou must be on your journey back to where you belong... the
powers of the medallion that you carry cannot change what must be done...
only the Father can alter that...T H I S must be done... remember .... what
your eyes have seen... what your ears have heard and the love in your
heart. You must live as He has commanded. He dies so that you can live!
Her mind went blank again and she trembled with fear at the thoughts in
her mind.

Before she wished herself back to 1955, she wished.... if only a wet sponge,
filled with cool water could wipe His face... I wish that this could be so.

A wet sponge moved across the face of Jesus and immediately turned red and fell to the foot of the cross. Red blood seeped out of the sponge and ran across the ground. Some of the Roman soldiers turned away and fled.

Jesus turned His head and looked at her and she knew instantly, that she was interfering with the destiny that only God could alter and she knew that she had better get out of there before the powers of the medallion were taken away. She wished herself back to 1955, at her apartment in Colorado and in an instant, she was there.

She reflected on what she had just wittnessed and she wept uncontrolled and trembled with fear, but then she was filled with a great peace and an abundance of love in her heart. The meeting that she had just had.... face to face with Jesus Christ.... the image of His face.... especially His eyes, was engraved into her mind, forever.

Marla completed her graduate work with Honors and now, she was free to join her father. But during the three months of Summer, she had read the Bible and anything else that she could get her hands on, as she had studied about the life of Jesus.

She joined her father in the Valley of the Kings in the Nile River region and she explained the whole story to him. He didn't believe her; thinking that she had been out in the sun too long until she proved it to him. She wished them back to the United States - to the steps of the Library of Congress and then back to the Nile Valley, before he believed her. She told her father, how she had wiped the face of Jesus, but nothing had happened. He asked to see the scarf and she showed it to him. There was no physical evidence present on the scarf.... no blood anywhere, but he had it tested and analized anyhow. When the test results came back, all of the technicians were shocked.

There was a smear of blood on the cloth, that was assessed as having been almost two thousand years old. The technicians asked alot of questions but her father dismmissed them and put off their questions. Marla had the scarf put in an airtight, glassed container and then labeled it, "Blood of Jesus Christ". The next day, she wished herself to the Vatican and gave the box to Vatican Historians, telling them that it was true.... the Blood of Jesus Christ. To trust her and have the cloth tested. She disappeared right before their eyes. Later, tests confirmed that what she had told them was a confirmed truth. Her father was tempted to use the medallion to help him locate the great lost treasures of the ancient world in the region. But he was a Christian and a man of great pride and his ethics were beyond reproach and he refused to use the medallion that way or let his daughter help him find lost tombs or cities from past civilizations.

Instead, they both took a one year leave of absence and together, they traveled the world, hopping from one time zone to another. They witnessed the ancient civiizations of Egypt, China and Europe. They observed chariot races in Rome. They witnessed great battles betweeen Messenia and Sparta. They saw Nero and heard his terrible off-key singing. They watched ancient Rome burn to the ground. Centuries later, they stood on the site where Jesus had hung on the cross and stood in the cave where He had been buried; the burning flash marks still etched in the stone walls of the cave. They stood on a hilltop, overlooking the Battle of Waterloo and watched the defeat of Napoleon. They were on the Mayflower when it beached at Plymouth Rock. They witnessed the arguing by the early Representatives of the original Thirteen Colonies as they sought the final drafts of the Constitution Bill and saw Benjamin Franklin sign it.

They were on the boat, when Washington crossed the Delaware with his troops, experiencing the cold and hunger that the troops did. They witnessed Lincoln's Gettsburg Address and later his assassination. They were at the Battle of Bull Run and saw the terrible fighting between Americans and Marla vomited when a mortar ball hit a young man, not more than sixteen, in the chest and ripped him apart.

They travelled into the future and saw great American leaders assassinated. John F. Kennedy, Martin Luther King, Bobby Kennedy. From the VIP Observation Platform, they watched the Challenger spacecraft explode in a ball of fire and smoke, only seconds into the launch. The two of them marveled at the color television, video recorders, computers; all of the electronic wonders of the home. They felt the air conditioned air and witnessed the cars and planes of the 80's.

They traveled thru the turn of the century 2000 and beyond, facinated by jet travel to Europe in a few hours and passenger space shuttles to the moon and outer space planets. Glider cars that hovered near the ground and sped along quickly, guided by computers and guidance systems.
They went to the edge of the year 3000; Dec. 31, 2999 and peeked into the future, but as the time zone approached them, all that they saw was darkness and they quickly wished themselves back to 1955.

The greatest observation that Marla's father had experienced, was when they had walked through a museum in New York in 1995 and they saw treasures and artifacts from the long lost city of Atlantis. The information cards listed a Dr. Carl Rowler as the discovery archeologist of the lost city. He knew that he must have found it on his own, as he had refused to use the medallion.

Carl went back to his work in the Nile Valley. Marla had never been the same since she had seen the face of Jesus Christ and she performed wishes for mankind, wherever she could help them save their souls. One night, Marla had a vision or a dream. Her dream told her that she must pass the medallion on to a new recipient. She must put the medallion in a sealed box and place it on the eighteenth car of a freight train in the Denver railroad yard. Her time was completed on earth; her work was finished as was her dad's. That in a short period of time, they would be in a Paradise that neither of them could even imagine.

The next day, she placed the box on the train as she had been told in the dream and went back home. That night, she died at exactly 2:00 am; the same time her father died, only two blocks away. He had made a great sea discovery and rushed to her town, to tell her. It was late night and and he had checked into a nearby motel. He would see her in the morning.

The train pulled out the next day; the eighteenth car was an open, flatbed car, carrying heavy machinery and a small box vibrated under the machinery.

When you travel from home to school - or from home to a grocery or shopping mart, or run an errand and you come across a long freight train - with at least eighteen freight cars....maybe - just maybe -- this is that train -- with the little box on an open, flatbed car. If you see an open, flatbed car with heavy machinery on it's bed -- the Blue Medallion might have just passed by you!

Spook or No Spook

" Hurry Sally and Sara...they're coming...hurry and climb aboard " yelled Teddy as his twin brother, Eddie pushed the raft out of the shallow water and into deeper water with his long paddle. "C'mon Sharon...hurry Katie...jump on quick !" yelled Charlie, as he pushed hard against the heavy oar and the raft moved into deeper water. He reached out to his sisters and pulled them onto the raft. Katie hung onto the side of the raft as the current pulled the raft out in to the mainstream of the flow. Her older brother reached down and pulled her onto the raft. Once they were all on board and sure that the raft was into the main flow of the strong current, they all ducked into the small shanty and closed the door.

The Dober boys appeared along shore and the six of them began to throw rocks, sticks, pieces of logs and anything else that they could pick up to throw at the raft. " C'mon out and fight...ya dirty snakes...stead of hid- ing in you box " one of them yelled as he lobbed a five pound rock at the raft. The children on the raft belonged to a club called the Cobras. The Dober boys were a group of roughneck boys; mostly brothers and cousins, that lived further downstream, in the swampy marshes and bottomland of Sugarloaf Hollow, a rundown suburb of Liberty Springs. The houses, or shacks were mostly shanties that had been quickly put up by the jobbers as they followed the drilling rigs into the Southeastern section of Missouri.

" You snakes...stay out of our water...ya hear me ?" yelled another one of the Dober's. The Dober boys called them snakes to put them down as much as possible; never calling them by their official club name, the Cobras.

The ten Dober boys, ranging in age from 14 to 18, had moved into the area with the six families that followed the drilling crews all over the United States and they did not have much time for schools. They were c onstantly drinking, swearing and fighting amongst themselves, when they were not heckling someone else.The b oys had been in the area for six months now. They just stepped in and took over the lagoon, off to the side of the creek, just like they took over the area forestland and all of the swamp. Any-one who fished, hunted, swam, boated, or even walked in the area, was trespassing and the Dober boys were quick to step in and chase them off.

They did not fight fairly and all ten of them would join in the fighting against one or two outsiders. The young hoodlums were constantly in trouble with the school officials and the local law enforcement officials for avoiding school, drinking, stealing or beating up anyone who was trespassing into their territory.
The parents were just as bad as they lied to the authorities or hid the youths out in the swamplands until everything cooled back down again.

The current pulled the raft downstream and through the steep walled canyons of rock, safely out of the reach of the rock throwing boys. " We've got to do something to make those jerks stop all of this fighting " Sally said. " Yea...but how? I tried to reason with them when they ran me away from the lagoon...when I built the divingboard...six months ago...when they all came here...and you know what happened to me " Charlie said. He was a bruiser for a sixteen year old boy. Six feet-four inches...two hundred pounds of linebacker and wrestling terrior that was easy going and mild mannered. That day, he had punished six of the Dober boys with his pounding fists before all ten of them had overpowered him and beat him badly. He had been hospitalized for two weeks with broken cheekbones, a broken nose, several missing teeth and two blackeyes. But he had promised himself, that there would be another day, when the score would be settled.

The Cobras had met with ther Dober boys only three weeks before, in an effort to settle the problem peacefully and permanently. They had invited the Dober boys down to the lagoon, in a gesture of peace and goodwill and had told them that the Dober boys could use the lagoon on Sundays, Mondays, Wednesdays and Fridays and the Cobras would use the lagoon on Tuesdays, Thursdays and Saturdays.

The Dober boys had laughed at them and said that they would use the lagoon, any damn time that they pleased. The rowdy boys had punched several of the Cobras in the face and pitched all of the female members of the Cobras into the lake. Then they had went into a swearing, drinking, destructive rage and ripped out the diving board; cut up the deeper water warning rope and threw it into the trees; and set the sturdy raft on fire.

The Cobra's had stayed away from the lagoon for several weeks now and had finally decided to sneak down and repair the raft; diving board; and install a new flotation rope around the deeper water. Two members of the Cobra's; Eddie and Sara, had distracted the mean gang away fom the the swimming hole, by setting off firecrackers on the other side of the swamp and then hid in barrels, dug into the ground and covered with support lids and a covering of swamp moss.

Now the Dober boys ripped up the lagoon's diving board and cut the flotation ropes and threw them into a bonfire and walked off laughing, drinking cans of beer and throwing the cans into the lagoon or woods. "Let's come back tonight...we burn that damn raft good tonight....see...maybe set the whole woods ta fire" one of them said and they all laughed as they walked brazenly through the woods.

The 520 freight train roared through the valley and slowed as it approached the old truss bridge, before it crossed the old wooden bridge and then sped up, gaining speed to climb the steep grade on the other side. The Dober boys stood on the side of the bridge, waiting to jump on the slow moving cars and hitch a ride to some other town, where they could gang up on some unsuspecting victim and bully him or her into some conniving, take advantage, type activity to their advantage.

The eighteenth railcar; a flatbed car, carried heavy mining equipment and the Dober boys piled onto the flatbed, kicking off a small cardboard box siiting in the corner and watched it sail into the stream below, where the fast moving current carried it away. The gang waited until the train was nearly to the top of the steep grade summit, before they disconnected the railcars behind them, laughing as the disconnected cars raced down the steep grade backwards.

The Cobra's returned to the lagoon and once again, posted sentries, as they put out the fires and tried to repair the damage. Charlie dove off the anchored raft, from out in the middle of the stream and retrieved a small box, floating in the current and climbed back on the raft. "Hey you guys... I found something in the water" he exclaimed as he opened the box. "What is it? Open it!" they called out to him from shore. "It's some sort of coin or medal or something... I think that it is gold... and it has some sort of writing or signs on it... come and look. There are four points sticking out...and it has some sort of jewel or something in the in the middle and...w o w... it flashes a blue light... see? " he called out to the rest of the gang on shore. He held it high in the air for them to see. Everyone ran or dove into the water and swam to the raft and climbed aboard to take a look. "Careful...don't drop it in the water" Sally said. They all gathered around Charlie and each of them, took turns handling the strange medal, looking at both sides.

"What is it? What's that blue light? What do these drawings and signs mean? Is it gold?" they all asked as they studied the strange piece of metal and then the soggy, cardboard box..

They were not able to figure out the shiny gold piece of metal, with the soft, glowing blue light in the middle. They all agreed, that Charlie would keep the gold-like coin with him. Afterall, he had found it and besides, he was the leader of the Cobra's.

They separated for the night and Eddie and Teddy headed down one path through the woods; while the two sisters, Sally and Sara took another. Charlie, Sharon and Katie took the third path and headed home. All of them were in their mid to late teens and lived near each other, in the same neighborhood. They didn't have to worry about the Dober boys in this neighborhood. The local police had warned the Dober boys to stay out of the peaceful, well kept neighborhood. After terrorizing the town when the Dober's first arrived, they had been told to stay out and away from the area or they would be immediately arrested.

Charlie handled the coin in his pocket as they walked through the woods, following the path which ended at their backyard. "I wish that we could do something about those rowdy, old Dober boys" Sharon said. "Yea... they are a bunch of meanies" agreed Katie. Charlie continued to fondle the metal in his pocket as he followed his sisters. "I wish that there was something that the police could do... like arrest all of them and throw away the key" Charlie agreed. He felt the warmth of the metal and he pulled it from his pocket and looked at it, startled by the sudden warmth of the metal, but he said nothing to his sisters. They walked into their backyard and headed for the house.

The local Police, the State Patrol and the Railroad Enforcement Agency officials surrounded the village of shanties, down at Sugarloaf Hollow and arrested all ten boys on suspicion of tampering with railroad equipment, endangering human life and railroad equipment. As the ten boys were loaded into a police van, the parents swore and hollered at the law enforcement officials and one of the parents yelled, "we'll have them out of jail... damn soon... ya hear me... we'll get our lawyer and he'll be down there to get our boys... ya hear me?"

Down at the city jail, the boys were herded into a large cell and one by one, were taken into a nearby room and finger-printed and their photo taken. When the task was completed, the jailer locked them in their cell and threw the key into a trash bin. Within four hours, the boys were released into the custody of the oil company lawyer. The boys would appear at a hearing in three days, when Circuit Judge made his bi-monthly appearance over in Liberty Springs. "Our people want no trouble with the local authorities. We want to co-operate with all of you. But you have arrested these boys on their reputation! No one saw them release the railroad cars! No one even saw them near the train" the lawyer had objected to the police chief and he had to release them. The police looked all over the place for the cell key, finally finding it in the trash bin. The jailer was puzzled, as to why, he had thrown away the key, into the trash bin.

The next day, the whole Cobra gang met in Charlie's backyard, sprawled on the lawn and talked over the arrest of the Dober gang, the night before. Charlie looked at the metal as he listened to them. Finally, he spoke, "I just wish we had enough lumber and material, to fix up the diving board and the rest of the lagoon, again". Sharon said "they'd just break it up again". "Yea... it's no use... we might just as well forget the lagoon... summer is almost over and we have'nt really been able to enjoy the lagoon... like we used to" agreed Eddie, disgustingly.

In an instant, a pile of concrete blocks, lumber and plywood appeared on the ground, in front of them, out of nowhere. "Hey... where did all of this come from?" they asked. Charlie shrugged his hugh shoulders as he looked over the marerial. "I wish I knew" he said as he looked at the coin in his hand. He felt the warmth of the coin and looked at it facinated. He began to think about finding the coin and studied it for a moment. All of a sudden, he had this feeling that this gold coin was a medallion, that granted wishes to the beholder of the medallion. He pondered his thoughts over, in his mind as he studied the medallion. "I've got this feeling that this gold medallion is, somehow, magical. It grants wishes to anyone who touches it. I want to test it and see if this is true" Charlie said. "Ask for a million dollars" Katie said. "Yea" agreed the other club members. Charlie grinned at his friends. "No... I've got something else in mind... let's try it and see what happens. They all gathered around Charlie, to see what was going to happen.

Charlie held out his hand , with the gold medallion in his palm and said " I wish ... that I knew what this medallion is ... I wish that I knew where it came from ... I wish that I knew what all of these inscriptions meant ". The group gathered around Charlie and watched the medallion closely . The medallion's soft, blue light continued to glimmer and Charlie felt the medallion grow warmer .

All of a sudden , his head was filled with thoughts and he spoke about them aloud , as quick as they entered his mind . " This medallion came from outer space ... from a space vehicle ... from the Andromeda Galaxy . There was a planet in that steller system , known as Borderia . The planet was destroyed by a star when it collided with the planet . A space ship was patrolling the outer corridors of space , above the atmosphere when the planet blew up , destroying all life on the planet . The tremendous blast of nuclear fusions and shock waves disintegrated the spacecraft and blew it into millions of pieces . The medallion is the only one of it's kind and is a pure grade of raw corundum asbestos , galena gold , polished and fomed by speeding through hundreds of solar particles streams . The four pins were formed by millions of electrons that pounded against the metal and reduced the size of the piece from two hundred feet in diameter to it's current size of three inches in diameter . This remnant was the brain of the planet , Borderia . The magic powers of the medallion is a result of the corundum gemstone , embedded in the medallion and heated to more than a million degrees farenheit for over three hundred years , before it entered into a vaccum , where the temperature was ten thousands degrees below zero . The markings on the medallion mean nothing now . It was part of the sacred writings used to worship the Supreme Being , but the drawings are only fragments of the complete inscriptions . The dark sun means that the destroyed planet was located on the back side of the sun star , from what we see " .

Charlie was shocked, as were the whole group, gathered around him and they all touched the medallion and drew their hands away quickly, as though they would burn themselves or freeze their hands.

The whole group was stunned by the words that had come out of Charlie's mouth, just as Charlie was. None of them were in awe of the details of the formation of the medallion, or where it had come from. The details meant little to them and they did not understand the magnitude of it's importance to science. What the group did understand and were excited about, was the fact, that the medallion granted wishes.

The group wished that there was a way, to get the lumber and materials down to the lagoon and Charlie repeated their wish. In a second, the complete pile of material vanished and they raced down to the lagoon. At the lagoon, Charlie wished that ten big, male lions would guard the lagoon while they re-built the diving board and worked on restoring the lagoon. He also wished that the lions would be completely invisible to everyone except themselves and the Dober gang and that the lions would not pay any atten- to the Cobras and would not harm the Dober gang - only scare them and chase them away from the lagoon.

Charlie also wished that a large raft made out of corrugated metal sheeting would appear on the pond and that a large hut building would appear in the middle of the raft... with a door... and windows... and sleeping cots inside and with a rain proof roof overhead the hut. Instantly, the raft appeared on the pond and they all ran onboard and looked over their treasure. At the suggestion of each member, Charlie completed their wishes. A high slide that reached out into the water; a dock to tie up raft; a deeper pond, clear of water lilies, waste grass and weed litter; a a nice, clean, sandy beach.

The cobra's heard loud snarling and growling all around the lagoon and they looked out the windows of the hut. Ten lions circled around the

startled Dober gang and they backed away from the lagoon in wonder-
ment, shock and fear and then they turned and ran off. The Cobra's
cheered and laughed and Charlie said "I wish the lions would chase
them all the way home". At that, the lions ran after the gang. The
gang ran down the road in freight, screaming and hollering about the
lions chasing them. The lions, invisible to anyone else; and people
stared at them, thinking that the gang was pulling another stunt on
everyone or that they were all drunk.

As the Cobra's lounged around the beach, dock and the raft,
later in the afternoon, tired from sliding, rafting and swimming,
they all talked about what they could wish for next. "I know "
Sharon exclaimed. "Let's wish for a hugh, old haunted house".
"Yea" agreed Timmy. "With scary monsters and ghosts, witches
and all the spooky things in a real haunted house". "With a hugh
moat...clear around it...filled with alligators and crocodiles". "And
a drawbridge over the moat" the gang chimed in. In a moment, the
wishes were all completed and a hugh, old gray mansion stood on the
top of a wooded, hilly region, near the lagoon. Dark storm clouds
loomed in the sky behind the house and lightening flashed, as the
threat of rain and wind storms approached the lagoon area.

The Cobra's walked up to the moat and alligators and crocodiles swirled in the water and snapped at them and they jumped
back in freight. Charlie quickly wished that the monsters would never
leave the house or moat. "Let's go in and look around" Charlie said.
They all looked at him and together said "n-n-n-o-o-o". Charlie
grinned at them. "Okay...listen then...I wish that none of us will
get bitten or hurt in any way" he said. "Okay?" he asked. They
all nodded and slowly walked up onto the old, creaky porch and

pushed the door open. The door squeaked, like it hadn't been opened in years and they all stepped into the cobwebbed room. Immediately, they heard loud laughter from somewhere in the semi dark house. Someone or something snarled and growled at them from behind them and the door banged shut. They all jumped and Sharon said "let's get out of here... y-y-u-u-k-k" as she wiped cobwebs off her hair and face. "Aw... c'mon... we're safe... we can't get hurt... besides... I have the medallion right here in my hand" Charlie said.

"I wish we all had flashlights" Charlie said and it was so. The group stood in the massive front room, flashing their flashlights about the room. There were cobwebs everywhere. The room was filled with old, musty chairs, couches, a writing desk and old laterns hung from the ceiling. The rough, uneven floor had throw rugs scattered about the room. There were several pictures on the walls and above a massive stone fireplace, a hugh picture, almost six square feet, hung above the mantle. They walked over to it and looked up at it. It was a picture of a sailing vessel with full masts, sailing on the rough waves of the sea. The dark windows in the lower portion of the ship began to glow and light began to shine out the windows. The waves moved and the vessel tossed and turned, swaying from side to side. The masts slapped in the stiff breeze and the coolness of the breeze filled the room. "Look... the water is moving... and the ship lights are on". "Feel the wind in our face... wow". "Look at the ship... it's moving" the group exclaimed. Over in the corner of the room, a piano began playing and the melody grew louder, as it played. They watched the keys move up and downward, all along the keyboard. Charlie walked toward the piano and fell to the short landing below, not seeing the two steps that went down to the lower floor. The medallion flew out of his hand and rolled across the floor with a metallic sound and they heard it hit something several times as it fell downward somewhere.

"Oh my God...the medallion...I dropped the medallion...I've lost the medallion...help me find it" Charlie wailed desperately. They hunted for the medallion, hearing chains rattling; rats squealing and heavy footsteps coming closer and then loud screams that filled the darkened room. They hugged each other and a dark form approached them as it came up the stairs, out of the darkness. It snarled and growled at them and walked right up to them and stopped in front of them. Was it a gorilla? It was hugh and was hairy all over it's body. It stood erect and growled at them and they quickly backed away, in fear.

They heard growling and snarling behind them and they turned and stood face to face with a fierce, large wolf that bared it's fangs and something red dripped out it's mouth. It's eyes watched them intently and he moved slowly toward them. "Quick!...up the stairs" Eddie yelled, as he moved to the side of the two approaching animals. The group followed him and they raced up the stairs. At the top landing of the stairs, a white, shadowy figure floated into view and fluttered in the air. A cold, chilling breeze blew down the steps toward them and they looked down toward the advancing wolf and ape-like creature. "We're trapped...what now Charlie?" asked Teddy. "That thing...or ghost...or whatever it is, can't hurt us...I wished that...besides...we can see right through it...quick follow me" Charlie said. They approached the flimsy, white, fluttering figure and the air became colder. A loud, high pitched shrieking filled the air and the group covered their ears as they hurried through the transparent figure, around the corner and up the last set of steps.

At the top of the steps, there were eight separate hallways and they ran down one of the middle ones. The hallways were completely dark and they ducked low, to avoid the heavy cover and entwinement of spider webs and large tarantulas spiders crawling through the maze. One of the hairy creatures dropped onto Katie's hair and she screamed "get it off ... oh please ... get it off ". Eddie ran up and knocked the big spider off with his flashlight and hugged her. They flashed the light down at the floor and looked over the spongy, wet surface that looked like slimy, green moss. They ran through an open doorway and slammed the door shut. Teddy, Sally and Katie ducked into a closet to hide and the floor dropped away and they fell, screaming in the total darkness. Eddie, Charlie, Sara and Sharon rushed over to the closet, shining their flashlights at the floor. Charlie carefully placed one foot on the boards and stepped lightly, at first and then heavily on the floor, but it held. He stepped into the closet with his full weight and the floor held. He felt around the walls but did not feel any openings. "Teddy ... Sally ... Katie ... can you hear me? Are you alright? Hellooo ... anybody?" Charlie called. From far below him, he could hear muffled voices and he leaned his ear against the wall and then the dusty floor. Now he could understand the muffled voices. "We're alright ... we're okay Charlie". "Where are you?" he asked. "I ... d-d-don't know ... maybe in the cellar ... it's so dark down here,,, we lost our flashlights and this one barely works ... please help us ... please come down ... please?".

   "Alright ... we will ... stay where you are ... you'll be alright ... stay cool ... remember ... nothing can hurt you ... we're on our way down now" Charlie said. " Did you notice, Charlie ... that there are no windows in this house ... no wonder that it is so dark in here" commented Sara and he agreed. There was a loud B A N G and the door to the room collapsed to to the floor. They flashed the light toward the doorway and a tall Zombie like character stood there, dressed in Arabian type clothing, holding a curved, saber type sword, in an upheld position. "A-a-a-r-r-oool u w w w " he growled and his green eyes glowed as he watched them. The gang cowered in the corner of the room and the Zombie like creature moved toward them, swinging the sword downward.

They quickly ducked around him and he swung the sword and narrowly missed Sara, cutting into the wall as it crashed intro it. The Cobra group ran out in utter panic and they raced down the dark hallway, towards the stairs. A two headed snake coiled on the floor, in a doorway near the steps and hissed at them. It's long, black forked tongues darted in and out of it's mouths and they could not get around them. Charlie opened a door and flashed his light about the room. "Quick...in here" he shouted and they fled into the room and slammed the door shut.

A glowing, shimmering green skeleton arose from the old bed in the corner and stalked them. His teeth chattered and the round red dots of lights glowed in the hollows of his eyes. His bones clattered and clinked with each step and the girls screamed in renewed fright. Charlie and Eddie felt along the walls, hunting for a way out, or for something to defend themselves with. As they pushed on the wall, an opening in the wall appeared. Charlie flashed his light into the opening. "Quick...in here...follow me...here's a stairway" he yelled as he darted down the creaky, old, broken steps. The stairway was covered with cobwebs, spider webs and globs of moss and stringy strands of some slimy substance that dripped onto the stairway and onto them as they all raced down the dark stairway.

Sara was the last one down the stairsand as she neared the bottom, something grabbed her leg and she screamed hysterically. She felt a ice-cold gripping hand around her pants covered leg and she screamed again. Eddie and Charlie flashed their lights through the open stairway and a witch-like character cackled at them. "Now I've got you...you can't escape me" and she laughed loudly, cackling through broken, uneven teeth. Charlie saw a board leaning against a wall nearby and he grabbed it and shoved it in the old witches's face and her grip on Sara's leg loosened and Sara pulled away.

Down in Sugarloaf Hollows, the Dober boys sat on the ground near a backdoor of one of their homes. They were afraid to go to far from the protection of a house and they dicussed what should be done. "T'ain't no lions around here- no how" said one. "C'mon- you saw em...running down the road after us" said another. "Well... how comes no one else sees em... my ma and pa thinks that I is crazy" said another. Still, another boy spoke "well... those lions or what ever we sees... don't come near here... less we gets near that lagoon pond... no how... we best... stay away... that ole place... lest we take guns and shoot down dem lions dead... I say. "Man... lions don't die by .22 shells...might just as well throw rocks at dose lions... ya hear?" said another. "Well, we knows dose Snakes are behind this some way... we's got to do something to get dose Snakes back anyhow" said another. They all agreed. But nobody knew what to do about it.

The smallest of the Dober boys spoke. " I walks down da tracks, by the pond... this morning... I not see any of dose ole lions... but I sees some old house... on the hill... besides the pond. I not know where it comes from ... but it there... shore enough... I sees it this morning". At that, all the boys began talking and asking questions, all at the same time.

They finally decided to go have a look at this strange house that had not been there before. No one had seen it moved there .. so hoiw did it get there? They would approach the house from the other side of the lagoon, through the swamp, in an effort to avoid the lions.

They approached the old mansion cautiously and they crept closer to the house for a better look. They moved slowly up the front porch steps to the front door and as they peered in the windows, they heard snarling and growling from behind them and they rushed into the house, slamming the door behind them.

The Cobra group of children, finally re-grouped and hunted for a way out of the house. The dark, damp and musty cellar had a dirt floor, as were the walls. They hunted for a way out without having to go back up to the first floor, where all the monsters were located .

As they groped around the dirt walled cellar, they found a small, dirt walled tunnel that led out of the cellar . Charlie crawled through the tunnel, trying to see where it led, while the rest of them waited. From out of the darkness, a huge lizard hissed and snarled at them and they all crawled into the tunnel quickly, escaping the approaching lizard.

Outside the tunnel, the heavy rainfall continued to fall and water puddles formed everywhere. The water began to seep into the ground and finally, into the dirt walled tunnel, where the children crawled toward the dot of light at the end of the tunnel. As the children approached the end of the tunnel, the dirt ceiling and walls began to slowly crumble.

They crawled and scrambled out of the tunnel to safety . All seven of the Cobra gang had miraculously escaped from the collapsing tunnel and raced home, away from the strange house. They had lost the medallion, but at least they were all safe .

Inside the house, on the first floor, the Dober boys peered into the darkness of the front room of the mansion and wiped the cob webs from their face and heads. One of them lit a match to see in the semi-darkness. They heard chains rattling; rats squealing; a piano playing, but no one at the piano. They saw the strange picture on the wall and saw it 'sailing ' with strange lights inside the cabin. Something growled over in the corner and the boys backed away, hunting desperately for more matches, but found none . They pulled and pushed at the door that they had come in, but it was jammed or locked and they failed to get it open. The huge, hairy monster snarled and growled at them and they heard the heavy footsteps as it walked towards them. They turned and fled in panic, scattering in all directions, becomming separated from each other in the darkness.

Two police cars, two County Sheriff patrol cars and a State Trooper car pulled onto the field near the mansion. They were investigating several complaints or inquiries on a strange house that seemed to appear out of nowhere, near the lagoon .
As the police and associates approached the strange house, they heard strange growling and gnashing of teeth. They drew out their gun s as they approached the entrance and went in, flashing their spotlights around the room. In a moment, a multiple of gun shots rang out and the lawmen backed out of the house as they fired their weapons . Nothing appeared in the doorway and the lawmen retreated to their patrol cars, radioing into their headquarters.

By nightfall, there was an assortment of

Law Enforcement officials, Federal personnel and Government Military Advisory personnel at the site .The local reports listed the complete Cobra club members and all of the Dober gang members as missing. There was great concern by the entire community, as nightfall approached.

Gigantic spotlights were brought to the site and in moments , the mansion was lit up brighter than in daylight. The plan was to conduct a room by room search of the entire house to determine if all of the missing children and young adults were in the house . They also decided to investigate the sighting of the stange creatures in the house, already seen and shot at by Law Enforcement officials.

Their efforts to discover the missing children was hampered by a multiple of monsters that smashed lights and man-handled personnel. The order was given to fire weapons and flame throwers at the monsters, but it proved to be unsucessful. Several officials were presumed to have been killed as they were dragged into the house .

As the early morning hours progressed, the monsters moved outdoors and into the darkness of the nearby woods and they repeatedly attacked the crews. The order had been to dis-assemble the house and the crews were chased, bitten and man-handled by the monsters . Soon, bulldozers were brought in, to knock the house down.

Several Dober boys bodies were found and rushed outside the house . Their bodies were ripped apart and one body was missing a head. As the day and then approaching nighrfall wore on , the toll of dead and wou nded crew members began to climb radically. Not one monster had been killed or captured thus far and the children were presumed to be dead. The order was given to burn the mansion down.

In seconds , the big mansion was a flaming torch and horrible, non-human screams filled the air.

As the house began to descentigrate, bats, rats, spiders, snakes and all sorts of hairy creatures began to flee the flames, many were on fire . By daylighr, a great pile of smoking cinders and ashes filled the dirt walled cellar. As crews sorted through the ashes, much later in the day , they found remnants of bones, both human and non-human. The bones were sent to the State Laboratories for thorough examination.

In later days, the immediate grounds were excavated. The indestrutible medallion was never found, though it had been scooped out with the ashes and spread out over the grounds. The medical examination reports came back andthe report confirmed that all ten of the Dober boys had been found in the ruins of the house . The report indicated that the boys had probably been dead before the fire, as skulls had been crushed; arms were pulled from shoulders; legs ripped off and bones with bite marks and pieces of bones missing .

The reports also indicated that bones found in the ruins, after the fire, were the remains of man-like creatures such as gorilla's, but much larger than the size of a normal man. Some bones found suggested huge spiders and lizards; others suggested hugewolf like creatures. Still others, suggested weird snakes and large frame, man, like creatures, possibly zombies.

The final conclusion of the reports said that monsters may have existed in the house, or may have escaped into the nearby woods, in the darkness of the night. But the final conclusion was inconclusive of that belief .

The general conclusion of the local communities was that monsters had existed in the mansion and that they had killed the children or caused them to be killed; that no one knew where the house or the monsters had come from. And finally, that some monsters did escape from the terrible, fierce fires.

Any one, stopping by old, vacant houses, sitting out in the middle of nowhere in the countryside had better be on their guard, for any remaining creatures or monsters that were now , known to exist.

The Cobra gang had escaped the terrible affects of the strange mansion with all its creatures and monsters, but they had lost the magical medallion. The Dober gang was gone now and the Cobra's knew that they now, had the lagoon, all to themselves.

Where There Is Hope...There Is Hope

Chris Lobell lounged on the soft comfortable couch on his front, open porch and puffed at his pipe. He enjoyed the cool, quiet tranquility of the small town as he gazed over the surroundings. Birds chirped in the trees as they told of a far-a-way rainstorm that was approaching. The waning heat from the July sun began to retreat as the cool, southeast breeze became more dominate and a rosy haze dimmed in the western sky.

A police car sped down the main street in front of his home, its red lights flashing silently as it turned the corner quickly, its tires squealing as it sped out of sight . In a minute , cars and trucks squealed noisily to a stop at the front curb, Cars were double parked in all kinds of directions. The men ran into the fire station noisily and their excited voices pierced the peaceful night air.

Before the doors were opened, sirens began to wail and scream at the quietness. As the doors opened, the flashing red lights winked at watching eyes.All five fire vehicles; 2 ladder trucks; a pump truck; a water truck and a electrical system/rescue vehicle sped out of the station. Their rear wheels burning rubber as they sped into the night.

An elderly man, crossing the street, near the corner, limped quickly to the curb to avoid getting run over by one of the trucks as they had not seen him .

Chris shook his head from side to side angerily at the display of immaturity and un-professional behavior of the men.One fireman gulped the last of his beer and threw the can onto a lawn, as he hung onto the back of the truck. A short time later, the trucks were back and put back into the fire station. Chris watched as the men reclaimed their vehicles, scattered all over main street and drove out of sight .

The town drunk; the rebel rousers; the
fighter; the gossip; the bragger; the conniving
home builder; the know-it-all hardware owner;
the holier-than-thou grain storage manager and
finally, the dumber-than-thou city worker. The
leading citizens of the community he thought .
All of them headed for the bar, down the street
and he could hear them whooping and hollering
from where he sat . In the morning, he would
have to pick up the bottles and cans on his
front lawn.

What kind of crazy town is this ? he thought.
What had brought him to this South Central
Missouri town ? What fate had crossed his
path in life and brought him here ? Was it the
small Colorado town from his youth ? That
town had been filled with loving, caring,
sharing, youth orientated people, who had
enjoyed life. Young, middle-aged and older
people had associated with each other, freely
and openly. Those people participated in all
the town acivities throughout the year, with all
ages. Winter activities in the snow , summer

activities in the park. Picnic's, swimming, open air movies and concerts. Town dances, all sorts of activities. Perfect settings in which to raise a family.

He had expected that similar activites occured in this town when he moved his family here. Here he sat , on the couch , on his front porch, on the main street of town, dumfounded, at what he should do. He had to trust his God and continue to improve his situation and not hide within himself. Keep his good humor and not get down on himself or anyone else. Unemployed with a family and no current prospects. But things would get better . They had to .

Chris finished cleaning the metal detector and got it ready for the trip that he would take with his friend Bud the next morning. Bud had called him and told Chris of the great lake in Southeastern Missouri, where the fishing was great and hardly anyone knew of the lake. Chris had agreed, but he wanted to take along his metal detector- just in case .

Supposingly, there was an old ghost town and cemetary near the edge of the lake. This excited Chris, as he was always facinated and curious of past old historical buildings and cemetaries.

The following morning, Bud arrived and Chris loaded his fishing gear and the metal detector into the pickup and they left the central Missouri town, headed for the lake in southeastern Missouri. The two and one-half hour trip seemed longer than they expected, as they were excited about the prospects of great fishing, and maybe a great ' find ' in the deserted area nearby.

They pulled into an isolated, desolate area in a region of standing timber at the edge of a huge lake. Bud wanted to start fishing right away and hurried toward the nearby bank. Chris grabbed his metal detector and began searching the grassy area, heading toward the woods and the building ruins, just beyond. Chris dug many false alarm items such as nails, bottle caps, pop can tabs and strips of aluminum. He picked up several old nickels, dimes and quarters that had been buried in the grass for many years. Chris moved over to a remnant old building ruins and searched the area. His detector buzzed vigorously and he stooped and searched the ground with a screwdriver. He dug up some type of medal or medallion. It was gold colored with some sort of blue stone in the middle. It had four points or fins sticking out of four sides and had strange markings or symbols around the edges . He stuck it into his sack with the other coins and decided that he should join Bud at the lake. They fished for several hours without any monumental success, catching a few smaller bass and decided to head back home. Chris was disappointed that he had not found any signifcant item, but at least he had a few old coins.

The next day, Chris cleaned and polished the coins. He was pleased with the excellent condition that the coins were in. He picked up the medallion and cleaned and polished it and the gold gleamed brighter from the medallion like coin. The blue stone in the center seemed to shimmer and glow, as it emitted a soft, blue reflection or light, that seemed to blink and twinkle. This would be his good luck piece he thought and he put it into his pocket.

As Chris lounged on the couch on his front porch the next day, he watched the town drunk walk by . He pulled the medallion out of his pocket and he silently wished that the drunk would learn to control his drinking or quit drinking. The medallion in his hand felt warmer and he closed his hand into a fist and leaned back and napped on the couch.

He leaned up from the couch as he heard voices and he looked across the street at the know-it-all hardware store owner; the town gossip and the brazen, conniving home builder. He silently wish that these people would be more Christian and not be so back-stabby and more understanding of people. He also wish that the town gossip would never say bad things again and quit back-stabbing. He would also wish that the conniving, cocky home builder would correct all of his cheating in his dealings with the town folk. Chris felt the medallion warm in his pocket and he pulled it out and studied it, wondering. As he gazed at the medallion, he wish that some employer would look at his resume with an open mind and give him a chance.

He lay on his back on the lounge chair and gazed up at the roof and overhang of the porch. God - he wished that he could do something to this old house . It needed repairs everywhere. Boy... he wished, he closed his eyes and napped.

His wife shook his shoulder and woke him up. He looked at her startled and surprised. "Chris .... look at the porch ceiling...there are new boards in many places. And come here and look at the back door... well...look at the outside porch door...and uhh...the inside house door...they are all new. I wanted to show you some of the windows...they are all new. They walked through the house, stunned that the windows and doors were all new.

The telephone rang and he answered it . It was a call from a local manufacturer that hired him over the phone, for the position of material and production control manager. He wanted him to start the following Monday morning, at a salary that Chris almost whistled at. He gratefully accepted the position and hung up the phone. It was several days before he discovered that the basement was like new. Not a damp, or low head ceiling with an old, broken down stairway as before.

What was happening ? Or had happened ? There had not been any workers around the house. Yet, it was all done . His wife simply shrugged her shoulders and looked back at him dumfounded, when he asked," what is going on ?"

He started his new position at the manufacturing plant and he was in his glory, at
how much he liked his bosses, the people
that he worked with and the building itself.

His wife told him about some strange
things that had happened in town and the
whole town was talking about it. The town
drunk, just up and quit drinking. The hardware
owner was being very co-operative,and
sensitive to his customers feelings and he
lowered his prices completely, by as much as
30 %. The gossip had quit the local gossip
club and spoke of everyone that he talked to.
The home builder was in the process of
contacting everyone that he had done work for,
over the last twenty years and acknowledged
that he had made errors and mistakes in the
past and wanted to make monetary amends for
all of it and he did so .

Later that evening, Chris and his family
sat on the front porch, enjoying the coolness
of the night air. The family talked about the

strange events that had taken place in recent weeks, but nobody could answer, as to how or what had happened. Obviously, some type of magic, or something. Afterall, houses did not repair themselves.

The medallion was placed on the top of Chris's bedroom dresser and soon forgotten . There was no way, that Chris had, of knowing about the significance of the medallion, or at least, that had been discovered.

As time passed, the youngest child came across the medallion and played with it. Eventually, the medallion was carried outside and lost in the back alley, where it rolled over to the edge of the grass. It layed there innocently, awaiting the next recipient, of its powers.

If I Knew That I Was Dying... I'd Say....

Steven Oliver climbed in his car outside the medical clinic and pondered the results of the rigorous test samples that had been thorougly and exclusively tested and analized over the past several weeks, from the blood, and urine samples and a host of other medical tests, that he had submitted to.

Now the test results were back and conclusively reported to him by the medical profession. Lung cancer; cancer of the pancreas, liver cancer and a large growth around the heart. The doctor had said, four to six weeks...no more than twelve weeks at the most. Steven sat at the wheel , dazed and shaken and wondered how he would tell his beautiful family.

His beautiful wife, Jenny, had insisted, that she come with him for the test results, but he had played down the importance of the test results, as being nothing serious, though he had felt in his mind, that the reports would be serious and devastating.

Steven drove to the city park and parked near the lake and looked out over the lake. He and his wife had parked in this spot, many times, years ago, as they dated . Here, they had shared in many discussions about life, their beliefs, wants, hopes and dreams and it was this spot, where he had finally proposed to her... where their lives together, had really began. It was at this spot, that he would tell his beautiful wife, of the short, time that they had remaining.

In the meantime, he must have strength and conduct himself with deep conviction and hide his feelings from his ten children and pretend that nothing had changed in his or her life.

That night, Steven took his wife out to a movie and later, a dinner. As they were finishing their meal, Steven jumped and twitched, as a spasm of pain shot through his body and his wife came to his side. He took several of the powerful pain- killer pills that he had been given and they left the restaurant.

Jenny helped her husband out to the car and into the seat. As she drove towards home, Steven asked her to drive over to the lakeside park, to their spot and park. As she turned the ignition and lights off, a chill ran up her spine and she was suddenly filled with great concern and worry. Steven looked out over the lake, at the nearby lights that shimmered over the surface of the water.

Jenny slid over on the seat beside him and put her arm around him. She touched his chin and turned his head towards her. " Steve...how bad is it ?... I've had this terrible fear for several weeks now and I have'nt been able to shake it... how bad Steve ? " He looked at her and studied her for long moments. She had changed very little through twenty years of their marriage. Ten children later and still the same person. Sure, she had the normal wear and tear marks on her face and body, but she was still the same faithful, caring, loving devoted wife.

Steven got out of the car, groaning with pain and she rushed to the other side of the car and

grabbed him and held him. He staggered
to the bank of the lake and looked out over
it. Jenny was behind him and she wrapped
her arms around him and leaned her head
into his back. "How bad is it Steven ?"
Tears rolled down his cheeks and he cleared
his throat. " It's bad Jenny. Real bad... the
worst, I'm afraid. " She hugged his back and
she wept uncontrollable. He turned around, in
great pain and held her tightly. They wept
openly and quietly as they stood there, hug-
ging each other tightly.

   " How long do we have ? " she asked.
Steven frowned and looked into her eyes for
several long moments. " Four to six weeks...
maybe twelve... at the most " he answered.
She hugged him tightly and wept uncontrollable. " Why ? ... oh my God... why ?...
you're only forty years old...it's not fair...
there should be at least thirty years more...
or twenty, or even ten " she sobbed. He
kissed the top of her head and hugged her

tightly and whispered, " honey... I love you with all my heart... I always will... no matter w-w-w-whhaatttt " he grimaced, as pain shot through his body.

Jenny held him until she felt his body relax and she hugged him. " When are you going to tell the children ? " she asked. He sobbed into her shoulder and she held him tenderly and lovingly. When he had regained his composure, he said " I think I should tell them right away... tonight even... you never know what will happen... or how soon... from now on " he said.

Jenny faced him and looked up into his eyes and smiled. The moonlight gleamed on her hair and her eyes twinkled from the mist that filled them and she placed her hand on the side of his face. " Steve... my love, my dream, my all. I love you so very much and I thank you for all the joys, happiness and love that you have brought to me and our children. I'll love you forever and I promise you that it will never change... now or ever.

Though my heart aches, from the short time that we have left... we must use our precious, remaining time wisely and productively. Is there anything... that you wanted to see or do, while there is still time ? " she asked, smiling affectionately and lovingly at him.

He smiled down at her and grimaced from the pain, until it passed and she held him until he pulled her away and looked into her eyes. He smiled at her again. ' There are many things that I wanted to do... and to see. There were many things that I wanted to accomplish... but my time is running out. I must go by my priorities now ... our priorities now. There are many things that I wanted to share with our children... things that I wanted to talk to them about... there may not be time now ! I always thought that I might outline guidelines for my children to follow... IF I KNEW THAT I WAS DYING...and if I had the time and strength... that would be my top priority. With your help... I can do this... I want

to get that done, Jenny " he said. " Alright...
we will... let's go home and break the news,
Steve " she said. In the car, Jenny leaned over
and kissed her husband long, hard and
passionately and kissed the top of his head.
" Oh Steve... I love you so very much...until
the end of time...I love you so . "

Steve and Jenny met with their children
and Steve spoke quietly, but directly and
openly, as he explained the full medical
details and the prognosis of his terminal
illness. The children all huddled around their
father and mother and all of them hugged
each other, as they wept uncontrollably.

" We must all, be brave and strong... put
our faith in the Lord God and trust Him... all
of you must be strong... for me and your
mother. Pray for me and your mother... we
should all pray for each other... and let's do
our best... with the little time we have left...
to enjoy each other and make these last
days... our best " Steve said.

" The children handled it quite well… I thought " Jenny said after the children had retired to their bedrooms. Steven nodded and the two of them walked to their   b edroom. They lay in each other's arms all night. Steven dozed at various times and Jenny smiled at him tenderly, as she watched him sleep. She had not closed her eyes all night, as she considered what Steve had said, .' I always thought, that I would outline guidelines for my children to follow… If I Knew That I Was Dying … and if I had the time and strength … that would be my top priority', he had said . She mulled the thought over and over in her head. She leaned over and kissed his chest and then his eyes. " My love … my life… I love you so! Dear God … help him with his pain … let him not suffer so … help us all to help him and to be strong for him. Father … I pray … that we all appreciate Steve, to the fullest … and that we use this time wisely, " Jenny sobbed and her shoulders shook uncontrollably. She placed her head lightly on his chest and he held her, wrapping his arms around her.

The next morning, before the children were out of bed, Jenny and Steve sat at the kitchen table and sipped at their coffee. Both were silent as each of them thought about the past events of yesterday. Steve considered how he wanted to approach his guideline, that he wanted to give to his children. He posed the question to his wife and she thought it over for a moment, before she answered him. " What did you have in mind, Steve ? " Anything specific in mind ?" she asked. He considered her question for a moment and then said " oh… I don't know … I guess that I considered a word or phrase type association or something like that. I mean …for example … love … or drugs … dating… sex before marriage … what it means to me … and how I would react to it. Or how I would advise them … if they asked me … or what I would tell them … if … I was there to … do you understand, sweetheart ?" he asked. She smiled at him, reassuringly and nodded. " Yes … I understand and I agree … why don't we get started on it and I'll write … maybe it would be a good place, to start with each letter of the alphabet … like A for absenteeism, at work or school, or A for abuse, or A for accuracy … what do you think honey ?" she asked . He smiled at her, " sounds great … that is exactly what I had in mind. Sort of an encyclopedia of what I might say or suggest to any of them … if they asked my advice on something … and I were here to answer them " he said. He came over to her and kissed her lips and held her. " Now, I know why I married you … besides the fact that you are pretty , smart, devoted and a great wife, lover, mother and most of all … such a great friend and consociate … my wife, my friend … my Jenny … I love you so much sweetheart " he said and kissed her. He trembled in her arms as spasms of pain shot through his body and he moaned and fell to the floor. Jenny knelt at his side and hugged him. " Are you alright ?... Steve … are you okay ?" she asked concerned. " I'm alright, really … let me lay here for a moment – till the pain passes. " They lay on the kitchen floor for several minutes, until he asked her to help him to his feet.   The children ate their breakfast and were told, by their parents, to keep their activities on schedule and they reluctantly agreed and they headed out the door for softball, basketball and baseball games that were scheduled for the day.

They sat at the table and worked all day on the list of words and terms that he hoped to use in his encyclopedia. He spoke the word and gave a short summarization of that word, term or phrase.

Alcohol – great if controlled moderately and one could say to himself, - I am a social drinker only. Abuse – to the body by drinks or drugs – Don't – be smart and use good judgment. Absenteeism – work or school – be honest and loyal to your employer – your school – do your best at everything that you do. Accuracy – always be accurate at whatever you do – mirror your best at all times. Aches – offer the pain and discomfort up for the honor and glory of God. Adoption – love the child as I have loved you – be fair and loyal. Keep your priorities in order. Afraid – trust in God – pray to Him – He is always with you – He'll listen to you if you talk to Him. Album – keep one current on your life and kids – you'll never regret it – nor will your kids. Allowance – never be ashamed to work for a fair amount of money for your work. Ambition – do your thing – the best   that you know how. Anger – okay if you must – but make it controlled anger – use good judgment always. Angler – fish and fish a lot. Take a kid fishing – enjoy nature often. Anti-Christ – Beware – trust in God and pray to Him daily – ask for His help daily. Anxiety – do your best – pray – and don't worry about what you can't change. Angels – they Do exist – each person has a personal escort at all times, to guide and guard us. Attitude – keep it positive and good humored. Be enthusiastic, ambitious and always cheerful.

They stopped their work and went to watch their children participate in the ball games and they both enjoyed the games and had a good time. Steven was taking more pain pills as each day went by and the pain seemed to intensify from one day to the next .

As the Oliver children rode their bicycles down the alley, one of the older boys saw something glittering in the grass, as the sunshine reflected the light. He turned around and rode back to the spot and searched through the grass until he found a medallion-like item. He picked it up and examined it, finally putting it in his pocket and pedaled his bicycle quickly, in an effort to catch his brothers and sisters.

As the days and nights passed quickly, Steven tried to keep his good humor and keep his spirit cheerful and the family participated in as many social activities as they could. They went on picnic's; went fishing; camped; attended baseball games; went to a circus; to several movies and finally, spent a whole day at an amusement park, thoroughly enjoying themselves. As Jenny drove the car towards home, Steven suffered a multiple of muscle spasms and great bursts of pain rocked his body. She drove quickly to the hospital and within minutes, Steven was hospitalized and given shots of morphine, to ease the pain.

The doctors examined him and confirmed that the end could be near. Certainly, within a day or two; no more than a week, maximum. His breathing was labored and rapid. His temperature fluctuated up and down. His pulse rate dropped and then slowly stabilized. The pain intensified and large amounts of morphine were required, to keep him quiet and somewhat comfortable. The Oliver family was gathered in his room and traded off, periodically, as they exchanged places with each other, going from his room, to the medical lounge, at the end of the hallway.

Jenny refused to leave his side and she sat in a chair near his head. She reflected on the activities that the whole family had shared in, the past two weeks. Steven had been able to share in all of these activities and enjoy himself, with relatively few outbursts of pain, throughout the past two weeks and she was confident that the children had really enjoyed all of it, as much as she had. She felt that all of them had gotten to know him so much better; to love him more; to become drawn closer to him. She was grateful for that! She was also grateful that, at least, Steven had been able to complete most of his encyclopedia, though he might not be able to finish it.

The Oliver children sat in the lounge, at the end of the hallway, while their mother spent precious time with her husband and their father. The children discussed the medallion and each looked it over. The youngest member of the family, an eight year old girl, picked it up and looked at it. As she handled the medallion, she wished that her daddy was not so terribly sick. The medallion warmed in her hand, but she didn't know. Down at the end of the hallway, Jenny ran out of the room and waved to them frantically, to come and join her. They hurried towards her. " Your dad just sat up in bed... he looks and acts a lot better" she said as they all went into the room. Steven grinned at his children and kissed each of them.

The children agreed to go home and get a good nights rest; the two oldest children; Mike, a sixteen year old and Marie, an eighteen year old, would look after the younger children. Their mother felt that the problem had somehow eased and the doctors had confirmed that his condition had miraculously improved and that his life was not in any jeopardy, for the time being.The youngest member of the family hugged her mother and told her, how she had wished that her daddy would get better and he had, right afterwards. She showed her mother the medallion and Jenny took it, looking it over on both sides. The older children told her, of the details of finding the medallion.

" Let me keep this for now. You children, go home – and drive safely. I promise, that I'll call you, if there is any change in your father… but I don't think that's a problem… I'll see you all in the morning " she said.

Jenny took the medallion in to Steve's room and showed it to him and explained the details to him. He took the medallion coin and turned it over and over, in his hand, as he looked at it. "I do feel a lot better now… how long that it will last… is anyone's guess… I only wish that we had all the notes here and that the notes for the encyclopedia were all completed " he said. He felt the warmth of the medallion in his hand and instantly, a pile of notes appeared on the foot of his bed.

Both of them were stunned at the pile of notes on the bed, that had appeared out of nowhere. They looked through the notes and Steven was thoroughly amazed at the complete accuracy of the meanings of words and phrases, as he related to them and his interpretations, that he had in his mind. Steven suspected, that there was some unknown power from the medallion and he studied it. He looked at the pale, green dress that his wife wore and he wish that the dress was a light blue dress. The medallion warmed in his hand and instantly, Jenny's dress turned light blue. She was shocked and she looked at him questioningly. He told her what he had just wished for, in his mind and it had happened. Steven, then said " I wish that each of us, had a malt; a cherry malt for Jenny and a banana malt for me ". Again, the medallion warmed in his hand and instantly, two malts appeared on the table, near the bed.

Jenny came over to him and smiled broadly. " It grants wishes... Steven... do you know what this means ?" she asked. He looked up at her questionably and waited for her to go on and finally, she did. " We can wish for better health for you. We can wish that you have a longer, normal life... we can extend our life together Steve " she said.

Jenny took the medallion in her hand and said " I wish that your health would improve and that your life will continue for many, many years ". The medallion warmed in her hand and an instant, clear thought came into each of their minds. There was a long silence and both of them, studied each other, as they realized the thought in their minds- probably from the One and only Supreme Creator. Tears rolled down Jenny's cheeks and she said " we can't extend your life, or even wish that your health would improve. The thought just entered my mind out of nowhere. Also, I had the thought, that when a person's time is up... it's up... and your time is almost up...within days, Sweetheart ". Steve nodded his head. " I know honey. I received the same message or thought in my mind " he said. They were silent for a long time, as each pondered over their thoughts. Jenny came over to him and sat on the bed beside him. Her eyes misted as she looked at him and a tear trickled out of the corner of her eye and rolled down her cheek. He wiped it away with his finger and smiled at her. " You are the greatest thing that ever happened to me and I love you more now, than I ever thought possible " he said. She leaned over him and kissed him and leaned back, " Steve, I love you so much, that it hurts. I don't know what I'm going to do... uh ... after you're gone...I don't know if I can get through it... or if I even want to...it's so hard to see you like this... oh Steve... what do I do?" she asked, touching his face with her fingers. He smiled at her tenderly and compassionately. " Sweetheart, we've had a great life together... we have shared our love as one... you must be strong... you are my strength. You must be strong and guide our children and love them, as I know you will. Certainly... I wish our lives would go on and on too... but that's not possible... God has His plan... all of us are a part of that... each of us live and die according to His plan... and I feel that you and I... do not have to look back with regret... we must look ahead with faith, trust and hope. I'll always love you… forever… if not physically, certainly in spirit. We must concentrate on the final preparation of my encyclopedia, while there is still time Jenny " he said. She nodded and smiled at him. " I want you to know Steve, that I promise to you, that your book will be done, just as you want… hopefully, in the next day or two… I promise " she said. They kissed and both felt much better.

Several days later, his condition took a turn for the worse and the family was quickly herded to his bedside and he had the opportunity to kiss each member of the family. Jenny lounged beside him and over his chest and kissed his hands, nose and finally his lips. He smiled at her and said " My love… my life… be strong… pray for me… I…love… you… I a-a-a-l- l-wwaa….." Steve lapsed into unconsciousness and the Catholic priest stepped to the bedside and made the sign of the cross over him. He had administered the Sacrament of Extreme Unction, several days before. The nurses were called in, and in turn, the doctor and he examined Steven. He turned to Jenny and shook his head. " He's gone Jenny… I'm sorry. "

Several weeks later, Jenny arrived at the cemetery and she put fresh flowers in the urn, near the newly installed headstone. Looking at the headstone, she noticed in the lower corner of the headstone, the words ' through my book – I live '.

There was no explanation for the phrase from the stone cutter. He had not put it on the stone and he went out and looked at the headstone, accompanied by Jenny. He was dumfounded, as to where it came from or how it got carved on the headstone. He turned to Jenny and said he would repair or replace the headstone. " NOOO !! I want it on there… that's fine…I'm satisfied with it … please leave it on " she demanded. He nodded and they left the cemetery.

Several weeks later, Jenny finished typing the last page of Steven's encyclopedia and took it to a print shop to have the manuscript printed and bound. Steven had finished his last wish… he lived… he would be with them , all the days that they lived.

Jenny met with her children and expressed her late husband's views with them. " Your dad told me, to talk with all of you, about the medallion. When we both discovered the powers *of the medallion, even though, it would not prolong your dad's life, or even improve his health, we decided; or he decided, and I agreed with him; that the medallion should not be used by any member of this family, for anything " she said.*

The children listened to her carefully and she glanced at each child, before she continued. " Your dad felt that the medallion could be like a god. That it could provide wealth, possessions, desires or wishes, that border on the level of godliness and he did not like this. He felt that to some extent, it interfered with God's overall plan. The medallion could and probably would interfere with the objectives, hopes and wishes of this family. He didn't mean, that all of you should not strive to do your best in school, in life and in all of your future's. Certainly, your dad was not against success, wealth or the attainment of material objects. He only felt that this should be accomplished through all of our own efforts and on our own merits – not on the magic and powers of a medallion. The medallion, in the hands of a person, gives them power, which may tend to place that person, on a level, that they may confuse, to be on a level with God. I agreed fully with Steven and we both agreed, before he died, that we would dispose of the medallion. Bury it, throw it away – I don't care how it is disposed, as long as it isn't handed to or given to a person. If someone else finds it, so be it. Then it becomes someone else's problem. But that was your dad's wishes and that is my wish... agreed ?" she asked.

The children were glum and solemn, but they nodded their heads. Jenny smiled at them and said " don't look so glum and sad. We'll be fine! We all do just fine. But we'll do it ourselves and with God's help... the way we would have done it, before the medallion was found. Do we all agree ? ...on your father's honor?...agreed ?" The children nodded their heads and it was agreed that the oldest child would dispose of the medallion... alone.

The next day, the medallion was taken to the top of a hill, overlooking a national forest and thrown through the air; and far out into the heavy timber, where no member of the family, would know, exactly where it landed. Though there was grief and dis- appointment in his heart, as he left the area, he knew that life would go on and the family would be just fine… with God's help… and their father's spirit … and his encyclopedia.

UTOPIA

Lana Owens strolled through the forest, following a game trail, as it wound through the deep, heavily foliaged woods. She frequently took long walks in the quiet, desolate woods and she thoroughly needed and enjoyed the refreshment of the quiet atmosphere. She considered herself to be a self-made naturalist; a lover of nature and wildlife, in this remote environment. She felt that everything should be kept simple and good. Common sense used, obeyed and enforced.

She had a problem with the lawyers of the land. There were lawyers that helped protect the rights of Corporations and companies, but neglected the rights or natural barriers of nature and wildlife. As Lana walked down the path, she thought about the iniquitous situations and conditions that existed all over the world. She pondered over, in her mind, all of the biggest problems that existed in the world today. Starvation; Sickness; Unemployment; Gun Violence; the Low living standards of the majority of people in the world today. The difference of opinions and interpretations by people and organizations, such as the Democrats, the Independents and the Republican political parties. Black people versus white people or red people or any other minorities. Christians versus Atheists; Hunters, Trappers and Loggers versus the naturalist, trying to do what they feel is right for the environment. People's rights that excluded women's rights. Birth control versus Right to Life. War versus Peace.

Lana stopped at the edge of a pond and sat on a stump and watched two beaver, as they chipped away at a good sized white birch tree, finally toppling it into the pond, with a noisy splash. She finally arose and turned, walking up the path toward her car. Something sparkled in the bright sunshine, just ahead of her. She left the pathway, heading toward the sparkling object. She searched through the dense underbrush and grasses until she spotted the object. She picked up a coin or medallion like object and she turned it over in her hand. The strange markings and engravings around the edges meant nothing to her and she wondered about the four points sticking out of the object. She stuck it into her pocket and hurried back to her car.

Back in her apartment, she showered and dressed hurriedly and put the gold medallion in her purse. She had one-half hour to cover the twenty-five minute drive across the freeway and she hurried out the door.

Later in the day, upon completion of her workday, she stopped at a supermarket, to pick up the few food items that she would need, for the rest of the week. As she shopped, she noticed a neat appearing, but poorly dressed black woman with several children gathered around her. Lana could not help but overhear the conversation between the woman and her children.

" Mom...should I get some potatoes? How about butter? Here's the fruit section... can we get some apples or oranges, Mom?" The woman was irritated at their questions and requests and answered sharply " N-o-o...put the potatoes back...we'll have to do without them until next time...and we can't afford any fruit right now...or butter...just the essentials...now mind...all of you" she snapped.

The woman was obviously irritated, that she could not afford potatoes, butter or fruit, Lana thought to herself and she was embarrassed and felt guilty, as she took two cans of cat food off of the shelf. She had heard the expression ' that some animals eat better than humans do ' and she looked away, feeling the deep guilt. Lana continued to follow the family, from a distance and she listened to the objections from the mother, as the children asked about necessary and basic food items.

At the check-out counter, she followed behind the woman and Lana was not surprised, when the woman paid for the sparse amount of food items, with food stamps. The woman crumpled the cover of the empty food stamp book and put it in her purse, as she handed the clerk the food stamps. " I hope that this lasts us for the next two weeks" she commented to the clerk in desperate frustration. The clerk smiled at her in embarrassment and nodded her head.

Behind her shoulder, Lana heard one man whisper " damn welfare system...giving food away like that...should make her work...like the rest of us...and stop having kids...cut her tubes...no need to have food stamps...it's a complete waste". The man he whispered to, nodded his head and said aloud " what'd ya gonna do?" Lana turned around, and nonchalantly, looked at the men. Both men had grease or dirt on their clothes and she guessed that both men probably worked in the huge, nearby factory complex, drawing an exuberant hourly wage. One man carried a carton of cigarettes and a case of beer and the other man carried a box of cigars and several steaks.

What a world we live in today. Everybody for themselves...the hell with everyone else, she thought to herself. As the clerk put her three sacks into the cart, Lana noticed that the black woman, also had three sacks. The clerk put the woman's sacks into a rusty, broken down car, that Lana had to admit, she would not be seen dead in it . The car engine started, much to her surprise and pulled away from the curb.
Lana followed the rickety, old car through traffic and towards the poorer region of town. She wasn't sure why she followed the black woman. Was it pity or heartache? Or was she just curious...she didn't know why, she told herself...she just had the feeling, to follow the black woman, and she did.

The old car pulled up to a broken curb, in front of an old, two story house, in the low rent housing development and Lana stopped at the curb, a short distance behind the old car and watched. There were several windows broken and black tar paper had been nailed over the openings. The steps were cracked and broken and several siding boards were loose or slipped out of place. The house needed painting badly and the small, patch of yard was grassless, as if pounded away by children, in an effort to play outside. While Lana sat in her car and watched, she remembered the medallion in her purse and she took it out and looked at it.
She was distracted by a loud voice, yelling and swearing and she looked up. " Dammit woman...you spend all my money for food...how are we going to make a house payment this month?"

he yelled at her. " Charlie... I only bought what we needed...and besides...I used the last of the food stamps...not your money. I know that we have to use that money for a house payment Charlie " she said gently. The black man was relating his frustrations of his situation to her. " I works sixty hours each week and earn two-hundred dollars. The state and government take a big chunk of that each check and my boss says I'll have to wait until next month, for my dime an hour wage increase. Yet he buys himself a thousands of dollars car and drives it four blocks every day. The damn President is on tv right now, telling me how lucky I am and how good I have it and that the country has to tighten it's belt and lower the debt...to overhaul the welfare system and make people work. If they would pay a decent wage...we would not have to have food stamps...without them...we would'nt make it...as it is...we barely make it now...and that is without any extras...at all. Ya know Lizzie,,,it's a damn shame, that our kids, or any kids...have to grow up in America like this. I'll bet the President eats steak or lobster tonight and we'll build and explode a billion dollars worth of bombs tomarrow " the black man concluded.

As Lana handled the medallion, she wish that there was something she could do, for this family. She wish that she could fill the complete back seat and the trunk too, with food sacks. Potatoes, meats, vegetables, fruit, milk, cheese, breads and all of the basic foods that most Americans get to eat. She also wish that there was ice-cream, pies and good nutritious desserts and food items. The medallion warmed in her hand and in an instant, she heard the black man yell at his wife " Lizzie...you tells me that you not spend the house money for food? Then how you buy all this food?...how come?" he asked. Lizzie took the money out of her purse and showed it to her husband and he calmed down and said " woman...don't knows how...you done it...but you's done good." Lizzie was shocked as she sorted through the sacks in the trunk and back seat. Lana smiled to herself when she heard the woman say " I's don't know how's I done it...no how either...I just don't know...has ta be the good Lord...is looking after us." The black family made many, many trips in and out of the house, as they carried all of the sacks inside and closed the door.

Lana pulled away from the curb and headed toward home, feeling content, satisfied and in deep gratitude, that somehow, she had, had a hand, in helping one family, to eat better tonight. Back home, as she handled the medallion, she wondered about what had just happened. Looking at a black car across the street from her, she wish that it would turn a color red and it did. She wish it would return to black and it did. Seeing a dog trot down the sidewalk, she wish it would turn around and cross the street and it did. She began to realize, that somehow, this magical medallion, granted wishes. I wish that I was in my apartment and she found herself sitting on her couch inside.

That night, she watched the news telecast on television as the President's speech was discussed by the news media. It sickened her, to hear how he had said that Americans were better off and how they would be better off, if the Congress approved his budget for a larger defense spending budget. She wish that she could better educate people, in a more positive manner. If people only realized how important their vote was. The majority of people, either didn't vote or they went through the motion of voting, never really paying much attention to what or who they were voting for.

Suddenly, a positive feeling came over Lana and she knew that she could do that very thing. That she did have the power to change the complete image and priorities of the whole world. She said aloud " I wish that I knew how I could accomplish all of that." The medallion warmed in her hand and in an instant, she knew the powers and magic of the medallion in her hand. She didn't fully believe it, until she tested those powers. As quick as she made a wish, a news bulletin would come on over the television. ' Russia announces that it wants to meet with the free world and the United States, to reach a complete peace agreement; Medical scientists announce that a vaccine has been discovered that will cure and eradicate all forms of cancer and most disease disorders in the world; Congress to unveil a new plan to feed the world and solve the unemployment problem! '

Several months later, Lana took her daily walk through the woods and she felt that she had made many improvements in the world. The wish that she had made about automatic fire weapons producers and the wish that they would comply with regulations for all powerful weapons, bullets and weapons of mass destruction was being fulfilled and completed. The government was issuing a plea to gun manufacturing companies to produce, promote and sell their high powered weapons, ammunition and accessories to government and law enforcement agencies only. No compliance by gun producing companies meant that the government would take the case to the high courts and pursue it – for years – if necessary. While these suits were on-going – the manufacturing of high powered, automatic, rapid-fire weapons would be suspended until a final decision was rendered by the high courts. Gun producers, under advisement from their lawyers, reluctantly agreed.

Sufficient federal funds to provide loans or grants to every college-bound student that was a citizen of the United States; job guarantee to every American citizen with an hourly wage of eight dollars for a minimum of forty hours per week; road and bridge construction; new housing developments; new federal grants that provided improvements in every Town, City, County and State, throughout the Nation. The funding for this giant project would come from a new crack-down by the government, to collect legal debts from unpaid taxes, enjoyed by thousands of very wealthy Americans, who in the past, had escaped paying taxes, with the existing, legal loopholes, that had now been closed. Funding would also come from new embargo taxes being imposed to off-shore manufacturing, that ships their product into America for re-sale. The complete reform of the total Welfare System that provides fairly to all Americans who need help. Grocery stores would exchange

Government cards that were punched by the cash register would be reimbursed by the government, eliminating the expense of food stamp processing. Americans would be provided with the necessary fuel to heat their homes comfortably. The difference that they paid and what they could afford to pay, would be subsidized by the government. The necessary funds were established by a taxation on American owned businesses and industries that produced their products   outside of the continental limits of the United States. When these products were shipped into the United States, they were assessed a special import tax and the tax funds grew rapidly.

A Special Trust Fund was established by new laws passed in Washington. Under the plan, the Money Fund Trust Account was to be built by the huge sums of money that was collected from drug busts and arrests. The money was to be deposited in special government accounts and held until the cases were cleared in the courts. The money would then be released to subsidize the Special needs projects of the American people, based on their needs and their ability to pay.

The plan provided complete health and medical care, doctor care and hospitalization to all people, regardless of their financial status.

The hooker, was based on their ability to pay back. All interested individuals and families would complete a multiple of forms to disclose their financial status. Investigations would be conducted on each person or family on their status in life. Social workers would visit the homes and conduct surveys based on their ability to pay and on their financial status, including stocks, bonds and investments.

A loud roar of disagreement filled the air in the halls of Congress and Washington, from the health and insurance companies, as they shouted that the United States was repealing Free Enterprise in the world of business. The government argued that billions and billions of dollars had been enjoyed by the health and insurance companies for many years and as these patrons aged, their health and insurance premiums were increased dramatically. The government would help set up individual businesses operating in the health and insurance industry and establish modest premium standards that would generate fair profits to the business, without gouging Americans.

Lana Owens smiled to herself, as she watched accounts of the new health and insurance plans explained on the television by the news media. Government officials headed off years of court battles, by conducting polls, all over the country. Polls were taken at fairs, town halls, libraries, shops, markets and in the streets of America and the results were vastly over whelming in favor of the government action – one-hundred to one acceptance of the new approach to the health problems in America.

Lobbying was banned from participation in Washington. Senators and Congressmen were now expected to represent their States and Districts, based on what their people wanted. An Amendment was finally passed, which gave each of the fifty states, the same amount of Senators and Congressmen, regardless of population; the larger population states would be allowed appropriate numbers of coordinators that presented the views on issues of interest, in their own states. However, these coordinators were not allowed to vote, or be an active part of the law making Congress or Senate.

Each State entity had an equal vote in the business of running the government. An agricultural state such as Iowa had as much voting power in Defense Affairs as other states like California, Texas, or Florida, where huge military contractors were established. California, Florida and Texas had equal voting power in determining Farm Policy or agricultural affairs.

Lana, now concentrated on the biggest project, that she was about to embark on . Something that would involve full employment to the world's total populations. Each participant would be paid a wage, in accordance with the standards in their own country. The project would be The Pacific International Transportation System and The Atlantic International Transportation System.

The Pacific project would start at Los Angeles, California and end at Hong Kong, China. The Atlantic project would start at Boston, Massachusetts and end at Saint Male, France. The tunnel systems would consist of huge re-enforced segments of steel piping with an inside diameter of 40 feet. Inside that pipe would be another re-enforced pipe with an inside diameter of twenty feet. Inside the interior pipe would be lights, fresh air ducts, exhaust ducts, heaters and equipment necessary to equalize the pressure inside the piping with the outside pressure. The best engineers and talent of the world would become involved in the monumental project. The complete project would be an ongoing project, probably taking a century to complete. With the two main trunk lines completed, smaller pipe legs would extend to various countries for maximum distribution.

Complete islands would be built along the isolated, lonely stretches of ocean, where no islands or land existed. This would provide access to service stations, motels, restaurants, tourist attractions and a multiple of business enterprises that would compliment the transportation system. Funding for the systems would come from a united world effort by all nations. The wealthy and elite members of the world would be sold properties along the way. The World Bank would join forces with all the Commonwealths and the American banks and all financial powers of the world to provide financial support. Funding would also come from millions of dollars in taxes, collected from all over the world. There were many, many bugs to work out in the gigantic project, but then, there existed some of the greatest minds of all time and they and all professions would be involved in these projects at some time or other. From the construction of the piping, to the waterproofing, the installation, the construction of the lines would involve machine operators, truck and crane operators, welders, pipe fitters, inspectors, and laborers. Thousands of professions from all over the world would be involved .

As a segment of roadway piping was completed and opened, a toll would be paid by the patrons. Percentages of profits by the businesses that sprouted up along the byways would be taxed. Later, amusements and other attractions would

Be attracted to the byways, all along the finished routes. The heart of the project would be twelve hundred miles per hour nuclear powered engine locomotives pulling eight one-hundred passenger cars, complete with dining and sleeping facilities.

Lana began to make the necessary wishes to start this massive project. First, a prominent planning commission to exploit the problems of such a venture and solve those problems with the greatest collection of talent throughout the world and provide a base of financial funds and backing, to get the project started. Her wishes included Congressional approvals and cooperation from the Senate and all U.S. government agencies, as well as the governments of the rest of the world.

Eventually, the tunnels would empty into a tree root type system destined for a multiple of nations. As this project was started, Lana began to concentrate on other types of world problems. She wish that Russia, the United States, the Arab Nations, Cuba and all other problem areas of the world would meet in a sincere, open and honest attempt, to resolve their different opinions and strive for a lasting peace effort throughout the world. As she made each wish, news bulletins began to fill the televisions, radios, newspapers and magazines throughout the world. The council met, with the determining goal, to eliminate all nuclear weapons from the face of the earth.

Lana was pleased at the complete progress of her efforts. The world, and in particular, the United States, was in a self-improvement mode that all people shared.
She looked down at the medallion in her hand and smiled. My work, my accomplishments are now complete. This medallion does grant wishes – possibly bad too. I need to put the medallion to rest. She returned to the forest, where she had first found the medallion and headed toward the lake. Standing at the edge of the lake, she flung the medallion far out into the lake, smiling to herself as it splashed into the water and sunk to the bottom. Her work was done!

Maybe some day, somewhere, somebody would find the medallion and begin a new experience.

Printed in the United States
By Bookmasters